How to Be Somebody Else

HOW TO BE
SOMEBODY ELSE

Miranda Pountney

JONATHAN CAPE
LONDON

1 3 5 7 9 10 8 6 4 2

Jonathan Cape, an imprint of Vintage, is part of the Penguin Random House group
of companies whose addresses can be found at global.penguinrandomhouse.com

Penguin
Random House
UK

First published by Jonathan Cape in 2024

penguin.co.uk/vintage

Typeset in 11.8/16 pt Bembo MT Pro by Jouve (UK), Milton Keynes
Printed and bound in Great Britain by Clays Ltd, Elcograf S.p.A.

The authorised representative in the EEA is Penguin Random House Ireland,
Morrison Chambers, 32 Nassau Street, Dublin D02 YH68

A CIP catalogue record for this book is available from the British Library

HB ISBN 9781787332102
TPB ISBN 9781787332119

Penguin Random House is committed to a sustainable future
for our business, our readers and our planet. This book is made
from Forest Stewardship Council® certified paper.

For Hugh and Virginia

. . . if you don't eat me I'll have to eat myself

FRANK O'HARA

PART ONE

One

I ❤ NY began in the seventies.

People loved New York before then, but they didn't know to
heart it yet. Hearting New York began with a doodle on the back of
an envelope in the back of a yellow cab on its way over to Madison
Avenue. The guys on Madison Avenue had been asked by the guys
at State Commerce to help put a shine back on the city, which was
cracky, crimey, whorey and basically on its knees. The Madison
Avenue guys gave doodle guy *I Love New York*, and he was in a cab
over to meet them when it dawned on him how to take that huge,
complicated feeling and turn it into something someone halfway
across the world could pin on a sweater or a hat and feel a part of.
He got it down in red crayon on the paper he had to hand then gave
it up pro bono as an investment in the real thing (he knew loving
New York). Before long, the city was getting back on its feet and
today makes untold millions licensing out that doodle.

That seems to be the shape of it, or as much as Dylan can piece
together through the wall of bodies at the Whitney, where the
original doodle is currently on display—tourists huddled around

it four rows deep, venerating, jostling for the best view of this feeling about a place. One man is on his knees trying, with his Leica Q, to rescue the idea from the glare of the real thing, which hangs just beyond the window to his right, violent with blue and half thought out compared to what's in front of him; stimulus and response, sealed behind gallery glass.

The blurb says that the guys on Madison Avenue came up with the words by talking to people all over the country and hearing repeatedly, *I live in New Hampshire (or wherever), but I love New York*. This is what's been used for the TV commercials, just everyday Americans loving the city from afar, before then zeroing in on Broadway and showing the stars of the big musicals of the day—*A Chorus Line*, *Sweeney Todd*—out and about in the city, high-kicking on the steps of the Lincoln Center, that kind of thing. There's a jingle too, which is just, *I Love New York*, sung over and over. There's a kind of locomotive energy to it at first, but when no one's listening, the muted words keep looping through gallery headphones . . . *I Love New York, I Love New York, I Love New York*. Desperate sounding. Like Dorothy clicking her heels, but as though it's Oz she's still trying to get to.

Dylan's only here because the agency is pitching for Tourism New York. The briefing was this morning, Saturday. There were small waters and small pastries and people from many departments. Afterwards, she was dispatched to this exhibition, in a cab. She's the only person working exclusively on the pitch, also the only foreigner. She is one hundred per cent Tourism New York. Seen as some kind of outsider, still, after seven years?

The bodies part and she takes her place in front of the scrap.

She can't deny it's a nice piece of design; a pleasing eyeful. The doodle guy, who's an icon-maker really—designed *New York* magazine, that psychedelic Bob Dylan poster—says he envisioned it as *a mini puzzle where you need to recognize the I as a complete word,* ♥ *as a symbol for an experience, and NY as the initials for a place.* He says the challenge for all communication is to move the brain. *This puzzle makes everyone feel good,* he says, *because they solved the problem. Also,* he says, *it came from New York. If it had started in Poughkeepsie, it would have died in Poughkeepsie.*

He was right about that, and about ♥, which started showing up everywhere after the campaign, like a new letter in the alphabet, X Y Z ♥. That must have seemed like a big deal, back when words were the thing. There are guards for the Hoppers and the Rothkos, but I ♥ NY has its own red rope too, VVIP, as though were it to go missing the feeling itself might disappear. Something in the torn paper and thick red letters seems to lay bare this threat, or at least let you know it's wisest to be on the inside of the feeling.

Belly to the rope, she waits.

Elevators swallow, regurgitate.

Outside, the day turns from blue to grey.

/

New York City can find its way through any earplug.

Its uneasy hum is close to the sound that used to come out of her grandmother's electric organ back in North London. She bought it for hymn playing and kept it altar-like in the middle of her tiny living room, beige and brown with gold, numbered

5

stickers above each key and a panel of fat, computerish buttons which made whole chords; black for minor, white for major. New York, through earplugs, is somewhere along that black row of buttons. You get the right hand too, coming in urgent and jazz-like, but mostly it's that background hum, that long minor note which lets you know things outside are well under-way, already complex and involved, while you lie there noiseless and apart.

A sliver of light, this morning. Violent, in the gap where the shades don't quite meet the wall. The shades are temporary, made of pleated black paper attached to the ceiling with a sticky strip. They can go for a while without falling apart, so she's got into the habit of replacing them twice a year rather than investing in some-thing more permanent. Set fourteen, this—or fifteen?—which pegged in the middle then droops to reveal the faded, red back-side of the artists' housing opposite, its off-duty air conditioners hanging haemorrhoidal beneath repeating banks of windows and the whole building so close she's got to crane her neck to get to blue. Her berth, her parents call the apartment. They like to joke about how she never got off the *Queen Mary*. Love this joke. She left London just after she turned thirty, which must have made it seem like a kind of marching towards. And now?

The sliver insists.

She pulls on jeans then a sweater; crosses Greenwich, then Hudson, then Bleecker and turns into the coffee place on West Fourth, where the server takes her name and, with his back to her, tells her he's opened every morning this week, which kind of works for him as he likes to pack a lot in to his day. He's working double shift tomorrow as he wants to get away. He's sick of his friends. His friends basically suck. Way too self-involved, you know?

She nods.

Begins to compose a fake text message—not even real words. This is strangely relaxing.

Faint trace of salt in her mouth, still, from the cravings that have begun to show up somewhere between no sleep and the feeling of being pulled, repeatedly, from deep sleep, just as it arrives. Noodles, usually, when this happens, from the twenty-four-hour place on Fourteenth. Specifically, that piece of pork they float on top, its perfect pinkness, which she does in two even bites while the guy rings her up. Now NPR plays through fake Monstera:

Things Are Happening In New York City.

She sends herself a message with the word *spleenly* in it and tries to summon a feeling of high stakes. Keeps this going as far as Washington Square, where a guy in three jackets slumps inside the arch.

Yup, he says, to no one in particular.

Yup, uh huh.

Otherwise, the park has not quite begun the performance of itself. First of the vendors, piling red fruit onto a cart. First of the dog-walkers. Couple of strung-out kids on the grass, still inside their Saturday night, looks like, not a part of this Sunday, freshly issued, single-use, wanting something from her that she cannot give. She counts out five singles for a bag of cherries and settles at one of the chess tables on the West-side of the park, most of which are still free at this time, first weekend of April, though it's strangely bright. The only thing in her bag with SPF is a stick of foundation, which is paler than her, like all of her make-up. Cosmetics people over here are always saying she's whiter than she is. Maybe they want an English person to be porcelain. She'll point out she's got some pink in there, but they don't want to hear it so she ends up with porcelain, thereby becoming porcelain and fulfilling the maybe-fantasy. The porcelain pushers are usually the same ones who say stuff like, I could just listen to you talk for ever, which feels good, if you're honest, when you first move over, then corny, then borderline fetishistic, though you lean in all the same, perform your Britishness, if that's what it's meant to be, sensing something to be had for nothing. A different proposition back home then too, hard to define.

She swipes forehead, nose, chin, then slides her laptop onto the chequered marble, where its rose gold glints like a punchline to the joke she's about to begin.

Which is the Get Smart.

The Get Smart is a document compiled, usually at high speed, to inform the uninformed on any given topic. The Get Smart will tell you how what you have can speak to what a person needs, or might need, or could learn to want. It will do this by reducing that person to their essence, by age, gender, $$, then by bringing to light the deeper yearnings and lackings that person carries around with them every day, discreetly, they thought. It's a diagnosis, of sorts; a vulnerability report. Scented suppositories are to acute piles as New York is to what?

A kind of trance state is required to produce this document, in

8

which its pointlessness is beside the point. She can usually achieve this quite easily but failed twice yesterday and can feel herself failing, again, today, in what was meant to be a no-plan Sunday. Part of the broader no-plan plan meant to leave room for something to happen. Or nothing. Or writing, which is increasingly something and nothing, feels more like a threat, lately, a symptom of some vague darkness waiting to rush into its place—I need to write, like tasting pennies before a stroke.

She sucks on a cherry.

Spits pits into the treeline.

A few chess tables over, there's a guy selling statues of Our Lady. He's got them set up like pieces in the game, an advancing army of blue. Every now and then he holds out a hand as if expecting rain . . . money? . . . a sign? If she squints for long enough, he starts to look like naked guy in that clip she's been watching, like the shelf-stacker at Gristedes sometimes does, also the teller at Chase. More of a short film, really, in which clothed guy leans over naked guy and spits into his open mouth for four minutes straight. 'Amami Se Vuoi' playing soupy, lyrical in the background—*love me if you want*. Shocking, for some reason. Addictive. Holy, almost, the way naked guy's mouth opens sporadically, incrementally, not wanting to miss a drop of what's coming at it. Late night, on loop, this works on her like a kind of wrong white noise. Or else makes her think of Matt, how sex with him is nothing like this, how aggressively tender. Not shocking, nor holy, nor anything new since he moved West.

Beyond the Marys now, the beginnings of a wooden frame. Part of that hokey installation where a passer-by writes down some story from their life, which is then pegged along a length of wire for the next passer-by to read, who can add their own, or not. All anonymous. Like a sad string of Western prayer flags, this thing, as it fills in. Swiftly, always. Something to do with that Woody Allen idea of New York and separate togetherness? Without the Gershwin, it's just communal loneliness. This is different to the solitude she's been trying to construct for herself since Matt left town, often by declining things she might enjoy for reasons she can't put her finger on. It's not pleasurable exactly and perhaps its motives are vague, but it feels like an expression of something true. As though she's making room for this. Mostly, it's just the same hunted feeling she's had for a while now, of the thing she is right at the heels of the thing she might become, threatening to blow straight past it and make her a done deal.

She squints at her screen, then the park.

Screen, park; screen, park.

This routine provides a sort-of relief, then after a while a sort-of high, then the strong feeling that she might puke; that it's reckless to attempt this exercise now, morning still in pieces, forcing her to consider the way a day is made, too, inside a city. A person, even, inside that day. She switches her laptop for the notebook she keeps for her own writing, which is the same as her other notebooks, but perforated; crude torn-out pages, like a used chequebook. She runs a finger along its rough edge, struck by how much she'd like to take some kind of a stand, but it's hard to say for what.

For now, just some small trace of herself on the page would satisfy.

Anything.

At work she would start with category.

This is an actual thought she is thinking—right now, this is her reality.

Fine.

Category: Human woman.

This seems vague.

The problem with this framework is she is both product and consumer, of herself. A consumer profile should be shaped by a clearly defined set of needs and desires as relates to the given product, which would then begin to give some idea of personality, ways to target and so on. She should be able to skip straight to personality in this instance.

A tighter definition of personality would help.

The Cambridge Online Dictionary offers the following:

personality
noun
/ˌpɜː.sᵊnˈæl.ə.ti/
The type of person you are, shown by the way you behave, feel, and think.

This is problematic, for two reasons—the first being the amount of groundwork necessary to establish behave, feel, think and the second being the idea these things are somehow fixed at any one time, either separately or together. But even if behave, feel, think could be pinned down, in the same moment, just for a moment, it's insane to imagine that examined together they would offer some kind of logical conclusion about the type of person you are.

In a behave, feel, think Venn diagram, for example, herself as the subject, there would be no overlap, no personality. None.

She'll try one.

Her first two circles come out as ovals, an aggressive slit where they overlap. She flips her notebook horizontally, this time using her cup as a stencil. A perfect circle begins to form on the fresh page, then a second, a third, while, either side of these, the table's checkerboard surface alternates squares of jet black and veiny, marbled white, reflecting, as if in a layer just beneath the stone, the outline of her own hunched form. To her left, a pale hand sits static, waxen, like the prototype for a hand. It takes a moment for her to recognise it as her own and, in this split second, she is completely opaque to herself. She observes the feeling, quite calmly, as it passes, then is struck by the sudden urge to revive it. To resist filling in and somehow empty out instead. She brings her right hand up to meet her left, the rest of her now spreading outwards into the park, over the blue trash can; over the girl by the fountain, knees up as though preparing to roll back; over the fountain's lip and on through the scoop of its dry bowl, up the arch and the tall towers beyond, rising up from townhouse uniformity into their allotted amount of sky, which is all about sunlight, in Manhattan—how much sky a building takes up, the shadow it casts. When that building is demolished, and all goes to plan, it falls perfectly straight, absorbed into its own footprint. Neat as hell, when you think about it.

It's dislocation she'd been looking for, in moving to New York. Perhaps she'd been thinking too small.

Two

It is Monday morning.

This happens every week.

The citrus smell in the agency's lobby has reached an all-time putrid high—forgotten lemons under forgotten limes. The two men whose job it is to produce this smell have already begun again, walking their industrial mops towards one another from opposite corners of the pristine floor, pre-empting dirt in a baffling system which requires them to be always cleaning.

In the pitch room someone is handing out the Get Smart.

I take it everyone's read the Get Smart? says Dan.

People have not read the Get Smart and continue to talk amongst themselves.

Something from the Whitney, then, to set the scene?

Dan is looking at her—she went to this.

She has three pictures from the exhibition: one of the TV commercial, where the high-kickers are so out of focus that they look like a spectral black mass moving up the steps of the Lincoln Center, and two of the doodle, both partially obscured by heads.

It was pretty rammed, she tries.

Moments later, an uncropped photo of a framed picture of I ♥ NY with half a head and a slight glare appears on the large meeting-room screen. The projector isn't warmed up yet, so the whole thing's also knocked back a few shades, like a faded postcard. The jingle follows in her brain, like a needle dropping onto vinyl and profoundly at odds with the energy of the room, already firmly in the grip of the creative team, Mick and John, who are in their mid-twenties and making faces like it's fucking stupid to be in a room forty-eight hours after the briefing. Mick and John are only allowed to make this kind of face on account of the many awards they have won for a soda campaign which doesn't feature the actual soda.

John connects his laptop to the screen.

Trump's a Cunt appears in a looping cursive.

We have this for print.

Okay, says Dan.

No image.

Okay.

Trump is yet to announce, but has not renewed his contract on *The Apprentice*, which is broadly agreed to be the same thing. *Nobody in the history of television has turned down a renewal*, someone, wherever, is quoted as saying. *But Mr Trump can do that.*

We have it in a billboard too, John says, then begins to scroll through a series of images with the same text mocked up on subway carriages, the big billboard over the High Line, a small internet banner, thus demonstrating its campaignability.

Dan waits until the last image to speak.

Guys.

Mick looks up from his phone.

What's the issue, Daniel?

The idea is to get people into the city.

Is it?

Or is it to make those of us already here feel better about sharing an Island with a stumbling jizzwagon?

It's the first thing, says Dan.

Yeah, well. Good luck with that.

I ♥ NY, head, glare, return to the plasma.

After a pause:

New York is Your Oyster.

The first of two freelancers lifts a board.

When the other begins to talk about the history of New York Harbor, Dylan would like to leave her body. She practises this skill the way other people practise meditation, but Mick is making it impossible this morning, forcing eye contact, willing her to produce the kind of strategic droppings that make a thing persuasive, that is not inherently persuasive. To crouch over his idea, right now, and make it winning. Or else he would like her to corroborate how the product is compromised. To unspool like a tired festival short—hokey-looking cast of locals mourns the loss of some place with a name like Hank's Fig Cookies, gone the way of all great New York institutions. Maybe there's some cello and an old storefront and it makes you feel kind of sad, but only because you choose to feel sad. You didn't know Hank. Maybe his cookies sucked, and that's why his store closed, but that doesn't matter to Mick, because Mick loves that the city is over. Mick has a massive hard-on for the city's deadness. Mick is going home tonight to put a cookie in a sock and pull himself off to how much the city is over.

A knock on the glass wall, before this can happen. There's a talk being given by a client at the end of her sabbatical year, and they need to show their faces.

Some hippie shit about whatever, says the agency's PR.

Anyway, it's starting.

They leave *Trump's a Cunt*, and *New York is Your Oyster*, and the head, and the glare, and join the group of bodies in the agency's central auditorium. Tiered seating on three sides acts as a sort of bleachers for all-agency presentations—prickle of influence, as would-be artists, writers, producers line up like sad bridesmaids each week and claim their part in whatever shadow of their ambition, snuck through on the dime of some big client.

On the stage, Anya is waiting to give her talk.

This is called Brand Sapiens.

Anya is like white Oprah. She is also like Victoria sponge.

Anya says good morning to everyone who shows up late and starts her talk with, Let me just drop this right now.

Anya has a monthly newsletter for creative people and others who are *high-level*.

Anya says oftentimes a lot, also efforting.

Anya talks about dialling down and stripping back, and only has pictures in her presentation.

Anya's helper does not know what these pictures mean or when it's her turn to speak.

Anya covers the mic to explain—everyone can hear Anya when she does this.

Anya asks a guy on the front row to introduce himself.

I'm Noah, he says.

That's okay, says Anya. She can get him somewhere.

There is a serious moment in which Anya talks about North Korea, then the change of algorithm at Instagram.

People are encouraged to write down the phrase *brand wound*.

Dylan likes the effect Anya has on her, which is like noise-cancelling headphones; her dough-like flesh; her round, tilted head; the way her voice keeps bouncing upwards, like a motor-boat clipping waves. When she stands up to leave, Anya is talking about becoming the model, or a model, it doesn't matter, because Dylan is already halfway out of the room, walking back to her desk, emptying her drawer into her bag. She is walking past the room with I ♥ NY and the head and the glare; she is stepping into the elevator, out through the lobby and onto Broad Street, where she stops for a moment to send an email. It says she's owed eight days of leave and would rather not work her notice period. She wheels her bike onto the East River Greenway and begins to pedal.

And pedal.

Past benches, bollards, rogue crops of sand.

Pedalling.

Into the bending cityscape.

Feet far out in front, impossibly far, river cut to shards by the sun and her motion.

Gear shift's thunk and whirr.

Brooklyn Bridge, Manhattan Bridge, Williamsburg Bridge.

Shadows repeating.

Broad Street far behind, shrunk to the size of a toy.

Thighs burning, clamped toes, tinny taste of blood—she bit herself when?—no matter because over the FDR, up onto Thirteenth, and something new to push against . . . Avenue C . . . A . . . First . . . University . . . left onto Fifth, opening out like a runway down to the park.

She freewheels.

Is freewheeling.

The sound of her spokes crisp, as if fed through new speakers.

And whatever comes next will be worth it, for this feeling alone.

Three

The apartment belongs to a woman called Anna.

Her profile says only:

Artist, Alphabet City

Anna does not do phone, only has a landline, which she's told Dylan to ignore if it rings. Her trip is last minute, a three-month residency at a gallery in Chicago. First choice had to pull out and she has a cat who needs looking after, for three months, rent-free. A freakish happening.

On the housesitting site, it looks like the cat is the homeowner:

Host, Anna, a Cat

Site's a nightmare, Anna said. Messages into the hundreds. She only read the first three and was happy to give the apartment to another artist—Dylan said she was a writer. And a cat lover— Dylan said she was one of these too, though she's never met a cat that's not an asshole. There's an automatic feeder, so the plan is not to interact with the actual animal, who is called Hopper. Otherwise, Anna says she should do what she likes, treat the place as her own, use whatever. Dylan said the opposite to the guy renting her apartment, who was still happy to take it on, full of her shit, plus mark-up. This, the rental market that awaits after *Host, Anna, a Cat*.

In Maps, she's already on top of the apartment, but the red door Anna described is up ahead, on the corner of Third & A. Through the red door, the backyard, where Anna has left a key, *underneath the head of Mercury*. This is sitting on top of an empty birdbath and much smaller than it sounds.

The apartment is at the top of the building. A five-floor walk-up, plus stoop. The stairs run in straight flights, rather than the usual doubling back, with just the one door at each level. This means Anna, *Artist, Alphabet City*, owns a floor-through Manhattan apartment. She'd casually mentioned the place was hers when warning Dylan about no super. She also warned her to keep her suitcase small, which she has not, now stopping on the third landing to shake out her hand.

Fist, fingers.

Fist, tiny-child-sized fingers.

Their smallness sometimes catches her by surprise. Matt calls them her Geisha hands, which he introduced on their second or third date when she caught him properly staring. His way of trying to convert an awkward moment into something intimate, like Geisha hands was the beginning of things they'd have together about each other's bodies, the start of whatever language they'd have which was just theirs, but—Geisha politics aside— you wouldn't come up with a cute euphemism for, say, someone's massive nose. Start calling them your witchy witch or whatever. And hands are just as personal as the face, even more so, in plain view at all times, right at the end of your arms. You barely know your face at all when you think about it. It would be more honest if Matt just called them her abnormally small hands. Sometimes he must feel like he's fucking a child.

She hasn't told Matt, anything yet, about the past few weeks. The thought passes through her head whenever they speak, I should tell Matt, like a song lyric or a line from a play. It's unclear why this hasn't happened, but it's been two weeks, which is long enough for the not telling to have become its own thing, with its own meaning. He's going to ask her to move to San Francisco, of course, will be part of the reason. Much stranger not to have told Sally. There will be a reason for this too, for her behaviour in general, being that of a person who'd walk out of the career she's been in for more than a decade, not exactly on a whim, but with no real forethought. This had not been true of her behaviour before and did not feel true of how she might behave now, the other side of the event, were she to have a job to leave—fuck, by the way.

At the top of the final flight, Anna's door opens straight onto a large living area, insanely large for the city, and flooded with light from three sash windows facing onto Avenue A. Furnishings are sparse: a chaise longue, Hitchcock-green, with a single spring escaping the bottom; closer to her, two oversized armchairs in a balding pink velvet, legs in the same caramel brown as the unfinished floors. The only obvious storage is a bank of low cupboards built into the left wall. Leaning over these, a tall, wooden ladder services the bookshelf running the full length of the same wall, and the wall above the windows. More books spill over into neat stacks around the room, one of which functions as a side table in between the armchairs. Large, hardback art books, looks like, with a lamp on top—Grecian torso, lightbulb for a head. What's the Rilke?

We could not know his mysterious head . . .

Incredible head?

Its final line—

. . . you must change your life!

Like a tiny bomb going off in the university library.

To the left of the living space, two doors open off a wide hallway. The first onto a long, basic kitchen, and the second onto what must be Anna's studio. Brushes, paints, rolls of unstretched canvas. Underneath a small window is the desk Anna said she could write from. Anna also said to use the paints, use whatever, which is laughable. It's relief she feels, mostly, in front of a piece of art. A happy compasslessness she's never experienced in word making; a process constantly underway at the front of her head, in all that congestion right behind the eyes, where thinking happens too.

At the end of the hallway, a mattress box, floor lamp and sheepskin rug have been arranged in the centre of a space only slightly smaller than the living area. Aggressively spare, but for a vast antique wardrobe pushed up against the left wall. Dark wood, wide drawers, vanity built in. Like a parked lorry in this set-up. The bottom drawer is open. She begins to explore its contents, gently at first, then with more of a sense of purpose as she moves onto the drawer above. The drawer above that. The vanity drawers are smaller, cube-shaped, three in a row. The first is empty but the second and third are filled with condoms, wrist-deep, and two giant tubes of lube. Really?

Anna, Alphabet City: Fucking, making art.

Inside the wardrobe everything is hanging, the thing she's looking for would not be hanging. She picks up the pace. Living room, kitchen, studio; shelves, cupboards, drawers. All a blank. Frantic, now, as she returns to the bedroom, looking for something—what thing?—that is vague, but must show itself eventually. Off the bedroom, a bathroom with a deep, freestanding tub offers a thing to do next. She strips, turns both taps to their extremes then adds a lug of whatever's in the caddy. This opens up, sickly sweet, while she takes in the piece of digital art on the opposite wall—a woman's face, photoreal, with a superimposed mouth, cartoonish, red, stretched into a disturbingly wide oval. Hung deliberately low, it skims the open toilet seat with a brazenness that makes her conscious of her nakedness. And dicklessness. Of the mouth's hunger, too. Extreme, it then seems, and impossibly intense to be touching nothing but water.

She slips her hand between her legs.

Can't focus.

Empties her lungs instead and sinks just below the surface, where she remains suspended, like an organ in a jar. Ninety seconds, a person is meant to manage underwater. This seems completely doable, as she begins to count, unaware of having taken much of a breath at the outset, not feeling she needs to when her body surfaces regardless, somewhere around fifty seconds, to the sound of banging.

At the door?

Fuck.

Easy enough to ignore this, but she's climbing out all the same, unhooking a robe from the door, disoriented, as she crosses the living room, and a little concerned, but mostly relieved to find a situation unfolding. Anything, at all, unfolding.

On the landing, a polished, athletic-looking woman introduces herself as Kate, then apologises for interrupting a shower.

Did she?

She slides her phone into the pocket of the black, mesh track top she's paired with black running tights. Somewhere in her forties? Brunette hair gathered into a slick twist.

They, she then says—Kate and—have just moved into the apartment below and are warming the place with a few drinks tonight. She stands close to Dylan's face as she says this, somehow aggressively engaged, yet also not quite looking at her.

You're probably going to hear some noise, she adds, but we'll try to wrap it up by one, two . . . somewhere around there. I left a note for the couple below—is it? Haven't seen them since before the move. Anyway, you should swing by, any time from eight.

Got it, she says.

She will not swing by.

Will you?

I'll try.

Bring whoever, by the way.

It's just me—would be, says Dylan.

Kate stops on the lower landing and looks back up.

Floor to yourself?

She nods.

Good for you, Kate says, then tilts her head, just slightly, as though taking her in properly for the first time.

Hey, maybe we can set you up tonight?

Something in the blatantness of this reappraisal stops Dylan correcting Kate about the apartment, or the fact of Matt. Instead, she arranges her face into what she means to be an opaque smile, but might be something else, or nothing at all.

And maybe she will go, just for a while.

Just to see.

By eleven, the noise below suggests a room she could disappear into quite easily. She's wearing a top she found in Anna's wardrobe, some kind of vintage robe, or housecoat. Oxblood red, lined. It hits just below the knee and hangs heavily enough to disguise the fact it's made for someone with broader shoulders. She's paired it with black jeans, black ankle boots and a white T-shirt of her own. Her reflection takes her by surprise; made strange not just by the long lines of Anna's top, like an extra leaf in her five feet seven, but also by the full breasts stretching out the T-shirt beneath. Matt convinced her to go back on the pill in January, despite the patchiness of their bi-coastal sex life, but she hadn't registered its full effect until now; the tenderness, sure, but not the size. Straight up, straight down, she's always been. Long-limbed, but in a way that's out of proportion with her compact frame and makes her seem more lanky than slender, like a provisional sketch for something more womanly.

Less so, plus tits.

Plus tits, the beginning of something else.

On her way out, she picks up an unopened bottle of Scotch. Anna probably didn't mean whisky when she said use whatever, or clothes, or the cologne she found on the shelf in the bathroom and has spritzed so heavily that it feels like another living being following her down the stairs and through the open door of Kate's apartment, where there are small foods, nasal voices, and no music is playing. Before she can reverse out, Kate separates from the nearest huddle, pressing a cheek against hers.

You came.

Kate repeats the cheek-pressing on the other side, but does not make a kiss noise either time, which confuses the gesture and makes it seem like she might be trying to whisper something or push Dylan over with her head.

You didn't need to bring this.

She scans the Scotch, front and back, then takes Dylan's hand and steers her through the packed room. The gathering, like the décor, is mostly sleek, mostly white. The only obvious structural difference to Anna's place is the kitchen, which is open plan onto the living area and working as a bar tonight. They're still holding hands when they arrive at its marble counter, Dylan lagging behind, like Kate's child.

Kate passes the Scotch to the bartender.

Rocks?

Sure, she nods.

She doesn't like whisky but is finding Kate's ongoing wrong assumptions quite relaxing. She accepts a heavy, cut-crystal tumbler, then surrenders to the kind of rapid-fire small talk she hates but has a natural gift for. This has just begun to gather grim momentum when a server appears at Kate's ear and whispers something. Her eyes widen, just slightly.

Can I leave you alone?

Finally, Dylan says—meaning to say fine.

Kate laughs as she crosses the kitchen.

If you need some air, a smoke, whatever, she says, and opens the fire-escape door.

Dylan steps through this, instinctively, as one does an open door, and closes it behind her. Crisp air fills her sleeves, her boots, clings to her face. She leans against the railing, tentatively, at first, then with her full weight, while light from the street mingles with her tumbler, hung out over Avenue A. She touches her tongue to the giant ice cube to see if it will stick. Thinks how strange and yet how un-strange it is to be there.

After a while, a lift in the breeze carries the smell of cigarette smoke over from her left. A guy up on the next half landing, visible through the steps, as if through a slatted blind. His legs are out in front of him, head dropped back. Something in the surrender of his pose makes her look away, but when she glances back, he's looking down at her. Light eyes under dark brows.

Does the smoke bother you?

His voice is low, southern sounding.

You're fine, she says.

He sends his smoke sideways this time, so that she can make

out a beard along his neck and jawline, the kind that comes thick and fast.

His accent is softer, more neutral, when he asks where she's from in England, as though he's made some small calibration.

London, she says, which is only half a lie, and he says he was at school there for a while, meaning university. Either way, this doesn't fit with the character profile she's already quite far into constructing.

Studying what?

Piano . . . jazz, mostly.

At your Royal Academy, he adds, mockingly.

I only stayed a semester. It wasn't for me.

How so?

I just wanted to get to it, I guess. Be playing just to play.

I can understand that.

You're a musician?

No, I just mean wanting not to, to not . . . to get to the next thing.

She often revises things as she's saying them, but it's not usually this obvious.

He makes a noise like mnhmn, then starts down the steps.

The railing vibrates against the side of her body and calls attention to the street below; staccato voices, doors opening, doors closing, cars going over the same manhole. He sits again, opposite side of the balcony, a few steps up, and she fills him in. High cheekbones, narrow nose, thick lashes like a circle of eyeliner around each eye, at odds with the broad shoulders and wolfish hair that make him seem more tough than pretty. Dark auburn, his hair, not the brown she'd first thought.

Gabe, he says, and raises his lighter in a kind of wave.

Dylan.

She manages not to wave back.

Welsh?

My grandad was a quarter, not even, but that's what he latched onto. Used to read from *A Child's Christmas* before the turkey every year . . . shocking accent—from the Gower, he'd announce, so you couldn't call him on it.

What's a Gower accent like?

Exactly.

You've never looked it up?

I like not knowing, she says, meaninglessly.

Why hasn't she?

It's an Irish accent undoes me, Gabe says, then flicks something from his boot.

She can do an Irish accent, a good one, but hadn't thought to answer in it. The idea is absurd, but there nonetheless, confirming the thing she could already sense when he only existed in sections.

So, what is it you do, Dylan?

He says this the same way he said Royal, like it's the kind of thing that might interest another person.

She leans back against the railing, less stable-feeling from behind.

I write.

Another half-lie. When she thinks back to her last attempt, it feels like a full lie.

Short stories, she adds. Mostly.

He doesn't press her to expand, only raises his glass, just slightly, in toast to her imaginary oeuvre. Closer to wholeness than her, somehow, in this gesture. As if on cue, the door opens, and the bartender appears with Anna's bottle of Scotch—she has stolen this and it's going to follow her around for ever. She offloads her glass, while Gabe gets a top-up.

Just a finger, buddy, he's saying, when a black cat appears and brazenly slumps across his boots. It looks as though he's about to scoop it off, but he flattens its ears instead, with his big hand, and smooths all the way to its tail. Standing above him now, she can make out a slight kink in his nose, the kind that's clearly man-made. A scar, too, a neat white diagonal in his eyebrow, which is otherwise perfectly straight, and fixed seeming, as though surprise were an impossibility. This feeling of slight violence is incompatible with the stroking situation she finds herself now crouching to take part in, hand under the cat's chin, tipped back in approval.

The bartender closes the door behind him.

I'm subbing at Mona's tonight, Gabe says. You should swing by.

Maybe, she says.

She will clearly swing by.

You came alone?

He looks at her with such directness when he asks this that the mutual cat-stroking starts to feel perverse. She draws her hand back and takes a sip from the glass beside her, forgetting that it's his, that it's whisky. She swallows, unavoidably, then heads back to her place at the railing.

That's me upstairs, actually.

Gabe's face does something unusual.

Before she can work out why, Kate appears, wedging open the door.

Honey, can you join?

Honey is unexpected.

Then:

People are asking for a tune.

Gabe, she's talking to. Working tonight, of course.

Kate straightens up.

Oh, hey, Dylan. Is this your cat?

Right, she says.

She'd completely forgotten about Hopper, who this must be.

He's a little overfamiliar, she adds, and the wrongness is palpable, of cat owner words coming out of her mouth.

Gabe presses his cigarette into a saucer.

I don't feel much like playing. I've got the bar later, remember?

Can you at least show your face? Kate says, and takes a sip from his tumbler.

No one's seen you all night.

Dylan looks from Gabe to Kate, and back to Gabe—it was a *honey* honey?

I was about to give Dylan here a light, he says. Then I'll be in.

Fine.

Kate nods a goodbye in her direction then leaves.

Gabe slides Hopper from his feet then stands. His long legs are exaggerated by the straight cut of his jeans and boxiness of the sweater which, too small across his shoulders, then hangs a little short, almost cropped seeming. There's quiet for a moment, as he takes her in too, presumably, arms stretched along the railing either side of her, wide sleeves like drooping wings. He knocks a fresh cigarette out of a pack of Luckys, walks over and slips it into her mouth.

I don't smoke, she says, trying not to let it fall.

Let's say you do.

He grinds at his lighter, which then flickers, and strobes, and makes a momentary cocoon around them. Noises from the party drift through the open door and she's struck by their startling irrelevance.

Don't mind her anyway, he says. She's just pissed I couldn't get out of work on the same night as her little shindig.

He says it like this—shin. dig—in the same way he said Royal and what is it you do. Like he's inviting her over onto his side of the line. The two of them there; Kate, the shin. dig, everyone else on the other.

He gives up on the lighter, removes the cigarette from her mouth and places it in his own, where he lets it hang from his bottom lip. Slightly fuller than his top lip, she notices, which is almost muscular in comparison, as though you'd be able to feel what he meant if he kissed you. As though he'd be able to let you know exactly what that was. He's close enough now to notice how pale, how completely without detail, her own face would be if she did not fill it in. Hair, the kind of white blonde that tempts you to imagine her older, to see how the pinched nose that's cute now will make a caricature of her then. Her long lashes, the same white blonde, invisible without help. A thick, blue line around her iris, the only thing to remind you she has eyes at all. Panicking, she pulls the cigarette from his mouth and asks how smoking is still a thing, instead of mentioning the thing she could have mentioned, that probably needs mentioning.

It's a relief when he finds this funny.

I'll see you at Mona's then, he says.

He drops the lighter into the pocket stitched into his sweater, which then sags, perfectly, as he turns to leave. Just before he reaches the door, his boot crunches on something—a snail shell? Louder. The sound travels the length of her jaw. He doesn't look down to see what it is, instead back at her, then raising an eyebrow, and the feeling is of something small darting across the floor of her stomach, disturbing things just enough for them to settle differently. She pays close attention to the shape he's making inside of her, so it's easier to recall when she comes back to this moment, which it's clear she will.

Later, he goes down on her in an alleyway, between walls of apartment windows, as the first birds began to sing and some junkie at the end of the block yells at himself about a broken zipper. They spoke at his gig, between sets, exchanged numbers, then as they left, he did something with his arm that made it seem as though he was about to twirl her, but instead he scoops her into this space. Now he's saying she needs to relax. You need to relax, he keeps saying. Maybe she does need to relax. Maybe she's uptight, an uptight person. Maybe that's been a thing about her until now, coming hard, ass pressed against concrete, smelling piss and old pizza. There are cameras, surely, around here? Or maybe he's done this before.

Well, that was a first, he says, and looks up at her, grinning.

Four

The mattress is memory foam.

Except it doesn't feel like it's trying to mould to her form, rather to push her out. If she's slept, it's only been for a couple of hours, running the night in her head mostly. She still can't get at the bit after the bar, which even at the time seemed to happen only in outline, but the fire escape replays in high definition, that feeling of space opening up, how she'd filled it with every wrong kind of word. Had she really said that thing about smoking?

In the kitchen, she pokes a hand through the cat flap to check it's working. No sign of Hopper since Gabe's hand on his back. Big hand, she'd noticed again at the bar, two big hands hammering at off-white keys on an upright piano, open-fronted, the kind that looks like it's playing itself—Gabe's presence some elaborate hoax. No singer, no tune she could recognise, coming from three musicians to start with, growing to six, seven, eight, as other people wrapped gigs around town. All of them crammed into the small space at the end of the bar. Not Gabe's usual jam, he explained between sets, but he goes where he's needed. *I go where I'm needed*, like it's a fire he's fighting. Anyway, she could tell the fucking would be good, just watching him up there. That much was clear.

She checks her phone, again, then remembers he's only downstairs, which gives immediate charge to the things in front of her—Tylenol, coffee, half and half. His girlfriend is down there too, presumably. She hadn't been sure they were living together until he walked her home. I'll head up to mine in a bit, he'd said, hanging back on the sidewalk. She'd half expected to find Kate waiting on the landing, but it was after five and the place was dead. Now she settles at the desk in Anna's studio. A strong sense, in this space, of that other space, career-shaped, nuclear-sized, that she's blown in her life. To fill with words, of course. A chance for this now.

Three clear months, for this word-making.

It's a relief when her phone pings to remind her that, at two P.M., in a bookstore on Grove, a Pulitzer Prize-winning poet will read from his newly published *Selected Works*. She's never read a word of his poetry but went to a seminar he gave when she was at university, on Yeats and his poems of death. He won't remember her, of course, but when she saw his name in the *Voice* a few weeks back, she got the idea she might remember herself. This is the only thing she has on her calendar for this weekend, other than moving in, which is written in caps and feels like it should have been a bigger deal.

★

It's pretty much the crowd you'd imagine at a Sunday-afternoon poetry reading. The fact she's able to observe this must make her something different. Another stereotype, perhaps, but not this one. She can live with this.

The poet holds a professorship at NYU and it's easy to pick out the students along the first few rows of seating, necks forced forward by that unspecific longing which owns you when you're young and someone inspiring comes into your orbit. In her twenties she'd tethered this to a university tutor. Walking his route to the faculty, when she knew he was lecturing, or passing by his study window, not looking to catch sight of him, rather to offer him a glimpse of her, then reimagining herself seen through his eyes.

As she sits, a diminutive graduate student appears behind a lectern and begins to list the poet's accomplishments like tired diner specials. When he realises the last fact is a repetition of the first, he waves his index card in the air, as if to erase both it and himself. The poet, who has been waiting behind a nearby bookcase, then surges forward and lowers his half-moon spectacles to make a joke. The audience laughs, loudly, then he does a thing she's seen other writers do at readings, which is to look at his book as though he's never seen it before. Holding it like a foreign object, he flips affectedly through its pages, eventually settling on a piece he says he wrote in his *very* early twenties. A knowing smile spreads like herpes across the room and she's struck by the peculiar energy which surrounds the certified Great Mind. How it seems to engender the sort of absolute complicity that's usually reserved for childhood. At a recent family gathering back home, she'd watched the next generation of cousins assemble in the garden and, in thrall to The Oldest

One, agree that the house was the castle and the end of the garden was out of bounds, and if you were wearing a T-shirt you were on this side and a sweater on that side, and if X happened you were in, and if Y happened you were out. The more arbitrary the rules, the more undeniable their author, the more faithful his followers. *But you're not in the game,* would drift down the garden, if anything came into question.

The main source of this energy is the student collective, who seem to rise and fall with the poet's every inflection, now midway through a piece made up entirely of idioms which he's sewn together into a sort-of sense. A yellow traffic light, visible through the window, seems to perch on his shoulder like some kind of futuristic bird, as the piece goes knitting itself deeper and deeper into a web of self-reference. The effect is pleasingly sedative and makes her wonder why she spends so much time worrying about what she has permission to write.

At one point, the poet explains, in a grave whisper, how great poems answer questions only they have asked. It seems likely his students have heard this before, but their chests inflate in unison, along with the rest of the room, so that for a moment everyone seems to float above their chairs, which is the thing they've come for, of course, to be lifted out of something, whatever it is they find themselves to be on a Sunday afternoon in New York City.

A cork pops, and signals the reading is over.

During the applause, the graduate reappears, lifting paper cups onto a plastic fold-out table, then a platter of crackers— each loaded with a single, comically tall pillar of cheese. She'd like to push his face hard into these creations, has nothing to say to someone like this, to anyone here, and is never going to remember herself to the poet, who will have no idea who she is and instantly see all the ways she has failed. She piles three crackers onto a plate and lingers by a volume of song lyrics, selected by today's poet. Meant to say something about the poet and the person who picks it up, offering little else of value. She leaves a mini cheese Parthenon in judgement of the book and walks out onto Grove thinking how everything is sales.

Everything is performance, too. Like the woman in the townhouse on her right, who's handing down a coffee and what looks like the *New Yorker* to a homeless guy attached, in a semi-permanent arrangement, to the side of her stoop, maintaining him like hallowed neighbourhood graffiti. Even as she's having these probably unfair thoughts, about this probably decent woman, she's walking into the café with the good Danish, that replaced something else, and she'd promised to veto. She's as bad as anyone, maybe the worst of them all.

What is your name today? the server asks.

Then:

Do you have any allergies today?

This line of questioning is at once energising in its suggestion that nothing is permanent, nor even certain for more than twenty-four hours.

$7.50, for the Danish.

This is insane.

She buys the Danish, which offers the perfect ratio of grease to finger to bun. Her sense of this lasts for two bites and by the third, she is filled with the kind of sadness that seems to come out of nowhere and is total. It occurs to her how much she'd like to talk to Matt, but also how she can't talk to Matt from within this sadness that is total without telling him everything else, or most of everything else. Better to do this face to face, when she sees him in a couple of weeks. At the party he's throwing. For her birthday. She really is a prize cunt.

When she opens her phone, there are two texts from an unknown number. Even the possibility they might be from Gabe restores elasticity to whatever it is she's felt hardening all morning, all afternoon.

Less easy with you upstairs, but we'll figure something out

This is the first message.

She wonders if she's missing some part of it.

The next:

Also, you should know I'm married to Kate, but it's not a thing. Better to get me here than the number I gave you . . . too much hooch

Married, but it's not a thing.

She barely has time to give this statement the disdain it deserves before a different part of her brain is attaching itself to too much hooch, enjoying the way it sounds, remembering details about the night before. And most likely she'll look back at this as one of those moments where she could have chosen—the ones she's always trying to hunt down after the event, when things have fallen apart. But it's a different thing, knowing that now, choosing it anyway.

Five

Edward has just called.

He was her first love; first real love. The one that was clearly for ever, if not immediately, then eventually, however many chapters in. Now he's her closest friend. She hasn't spoken to him in a while because he's in the final year of his doctorate, something to do with Aquinas and quiddity, which at one point she'd understood, and has spent the last month in a silent monastery in France. The idea was to work there on his thesis, but also, he explained today, to take a look around, as he's considering joining the order—becoming a Carthusian monk.

At a silent monastery.

In France.

Eighteen years ago, they dated for five years, first at university, in Oxford, where they were able to dream with the certainty of old stone corners, then in London, before he came out, or didn't, in fact, at that point. What he'd actually said was, I just don't think you're the one, which was not the wording she'd prepared for. They'd just started on the breadsticks when:

I just don't think you're the one.

The bread caught in her throat and she can remember willing herself not to swallow; ordering her brain to relax the muscles in charge of swallowing so she wouldn't have to deal with that particular arrangement of words. But the muscles contracted on their own, dispensing with the obstruction, and on life went, with those words still in it. He did come out later, with brave and honest words, arranged perfectly, just not then, when it might have counted for her as well.

After that, he was an actor for a while and an Ed, a singer, a speechwriter, an academic, and Edward again, always in a relationship after her, and now, maybe, a monk. About to plunge into silence and hand himself over to something large and cradling. It's not hard to see the appeal of large and cradling. Maybe even the silence. She considered writing their story once, but it felt like it would need to amount to something she couldn't quite get at. It had been formative, she could feel that, but any theories she'd tried to have about how it might have shaped her seemed too certain of who she was now. And anyway, there would need to be changes—where they met, family background—as it was too privileged a pain to be sympathetic. It wouldn't be enough they'd both been shattered like that, when everything was hopeful. And gay guy, straight girl has been done before, it's not new pain.

The thing that strikes her now, though, just after he's hung up, is how much choosing he's done. How many drafts of selves he's put into the world. It makes her own life seem like a string of accidents. There was moving to New York, of course, but she'd waited until she was thirty for that, by which time it wasn't a choice, but a necessity. Like mouth-to-mouth on a blue body.

/

Tuesday, mid-afternoon, Gabe asks her over.

Kate's in Marfa, prepping a client's exhibition, and Gabe comes upstairs and knocks on the door, without texting first. This is shocking. She can't decide whether his presence is old fashioned or hyper-modern, sort of post-social, but it gives her no time to prepare or think, or to buy herself time to prepare or think, so she just says, yes, she'd like to hang out, and follows him downstairs.

They go straight to the bedroom, which is the same as the rest of the apartment: stark, like a waiting room. She doesn't ask him why he's chosen to live in an apartment which is stark, like a waiting room, as that would be the same as asking why he's chosen to live with Kate. Which would be her next question if she was asking questions, instead of just thinking things. The kind of apartment she can imagine him in is much more like Anna's, which makes her relieved they've never met, as it was Anna's robe he'd liked, touching it repeatedly, in the bar, with the back of his hand, at one point with his cheek, which was strange, but felt good. Also Anna's smell, which he said was obscene, in a good way. You could almost say he'd gone down on Anna.

These are the things going through her head while she's

undressing in front of him, which are helping to distract her from the fact of undressing in front of him, while he undresses in front of her, on the other side of the bed, grinning, just slightly, whenever he looks up.

He rolls down a sleeve and asks her what she likes.

She has no idea how to answer a question like this, standing in a brightly lit room, before they've even touched. She's used to guiding things if she needs to, which she usually does, usually with her hands, but being asked to put it into words like this makes her feel somehow inexperienced. She tries to answer with the kind of smile that says he'll know if he's getting it right, but her eyebrows feel alarmingly high, so she stops.

Ideally the curtains would be closed, but she doesn't want to turn her back to him to do this, so she lies down and watches him instead, head propped up on a pillow, knees drawn up slightly, to flatter her thighs. When he pulls off the T-shirt he's been wearing under his button-down, there's a smell like petrol and sweat which makes her wince and flush simultaneously. His arms are muscular, lightly freckled, hair along his broad chest and shoulders. His torso is skinny by comparison, almost concave just below his ribs, and his legs seem skinny too, so that the overall effect is part man-thug, part boy.

She waits for his body to cover hers, but it does not. Instead, he lies perpendicular to her at the end of the bed and begins to talk, looking up through her knees, which are hip-width apart. He talks quite normally about his day, the gig he played last night, whilst looking directly into the most intimate part of her, or just over it. They stay like this for a while, him talking, her not

44

managing to swallow, or move, so that by the time he actually touches her—which he does first with his hand, casually reaching out, like he's taking an apple from a bowl, then gently with his tongue—she lets out a sort of high-pitched whimper. He grins and the whimpering carries on without her, becoming, when he stops to pull on a condom, more of a needy whine. She's ready to come before he's inside her, but he manages to keep her there in a way that makes her feel pleasurably anxious, then unbearably, so that at one point, when he pushes deeper, it feels like she might even be laughing. She must be doing something else, though, as he asks if he's hurting her, which, either the question or his voice in her ear, then makes her come.

Afterwards they lie next to each other breathing at different speeds. It occurs to her that she's usually touching herself at some point during sex, needs to, which makes her wonder whether she's remembered to touch Gabe. She was holding him, definitely, but otherwise has the sense of barely having moved at all.

That was nice, she says. Thank you.

His eyes are closed still, one hand on his chest, the other out to his side.

It was, he says.

Yeah, thank you, she says again.

He tells her he doesn't usually get a thank-you after sex, let alone two, then makes a joke about British manners, which is hardly original, but relaxes her about the touching thing.

I feel like I might have been a bit . . . I usually move around a little more, she says. I mean, I do usually move during sex.

45

Gabe rolls onto his side, eyes a grey-green, not the blue she'd remembered.

Really, I had a very good time, he says, then runs a finger over her brow in a way that is perfect. Somehow more intimate than the sex, this throwaway thing, which brings with it a sudden feeling of loss, as though she's already fucked up what comes next. This happens to her quite often, feelings of sadness following feelings of happiness. Sometimes they arrive almost together. His fingers travel on down her cheek to the slight dimple in her chin, that is not actually a dimple, but a small piece of floating bone. There since she was eight years old, she explains, when it moves a little under his thumb. She'd been trying a forward roll on the climbing frame outside swimming. Every Saturday she'd get close to halfway, then retreat. The one time she made it all the way, no one had been watching, so she'd done it again, more showily, and slid chin first into a metal strut in the grass. Her mother had been fixated on how it could have been much worse, her friends on the injury, so that the achievement hadn't registered at all.

Gabe grins at this last detail, like she's revealed something fundamental about herself, then explains he's got to leave for a gig. He'd ask her along, he says, but the bar belongs to a friend of Kate's. As you belong to Kate, she thinks, but does not say, nor feel in quite the way she should. This would be a good time to ask about Kate, and what kind of belonging, but she doesn't take it. She isn't sure what she wants to hear yet.

She'll ask when she knows.

/

They've been on Skype for half an hour when it occurs to her that Matt's voice is a lot like hold music. His face is also screensaver-esque, but you can make a screensaver disappear, so he's really more like something blocking the view. Which is also a part of the view. Like a lamp post outside a window.

It's unfair to think of Matt in this way—as a screensaver or a lamp post—because for a long time there was no view at all, then he was the whole view, now he's in the way of the view, all while remaining completely consistent.

She listens to him update her on work, the weird in-between temperatures they've been experiencing in San Francisco and something about squirrels in the Bay Area, while she nods, eats noodles and avoids questions about her own life. After a while he asks if she's listening and she admits she did shut down for a while when he started talking about Femtech, which she cannot believe is actually a name for a thing. He reminds her he's taken Friday, and Monday, for her birthday.

Don't make plans, okay?

She gets noodles on her chin while they're saying goodbye and he laughs and says he loves her. She has to read the back of the pot, then, to distract herself from the feelings of guilt she's been waiting to arrive, which are now arriving. After he hangs up, she finds palm oil hidden in the ingredients, as a subcategory of vegetable oil, so now she's thinking about a weeping baby orang-utan, but also how wasting food she's already half eaten won't bring its mother back.

She is becoming ruthless (or practical).

Also, there is palm oil in everything.

Also, everything is fucked.

/

This time, with Gabe, she remembers to move, almost pushing him off a few times, the pleasure is so unfamiliar. He says let me when she does this, and she feels her body weakening. Let me, he keeps saying, and she says okay.

Afterwards it feels like a wind has blown right through her, leaving the usual sad-happiness behind, but on a grand scale, like she's been hollowed out and it's the only thing giving shape to her body. Gabe's lying there, eyes closed again, one hand on his chest, one out to his left, breathing. This time, while she's watching him, she senses the room begin to tilt and her centre of gravity shift towards him. She knows this feeling, which is the beginning of tethering herself, something in herself, to a thing, usually a person.

After a while he's facing her again, saying she's beautiful.

I find you to be quite beautiful, is what he actually says, which sounds strange, in that way American syntax can turn surprisingly old school, almost theatrical—oftentimes, somewhat. It's strange to hear beautiful, too, which she doesn't get much these days.

Thanks, she says, again, then tells him how her mother used

48

to go on about what a beautiful baby she was, pulling out old albums, pointing at pictures, saying how people used to stop her in the street . . . such a beautiful baby. Always with this wistful look, as though it was a great idea she'd once had and never managed to see through. Such a beautiful baby. A sad refrain, like, I could have been a dancer, or, I always meant to travel.

Gabe laughs at this, really laughs, which feels nearly as good as the eyebrow thing.

Do you have a refrain? he says.

I don't know . . . I don't think so. Do you?

Not that I can think of.

Maybe you can't know your own refrains.

Maybe, he says, then pulls a bag of tobacco out of a drawer in the nightstand.

He walks over to the window and takes a lungful of air. It's just after six and there are lights on in the apartments on the other side of the Avenue, but he's unbothered, happily nakedly standing, then sitting, one leg hanging down, the other beneath him.

He begins to roll a cigarette.

I bet you were a beautiful baby, she says.

The banality of this statement makes her blush, almost before she's finished speaking. She'd like to get as quickly as possible to the part where he finds out she's clever, to create the conditions for that to happen. She's aware this is what conversation is for but she's too unedited live.

I wouldn't know, he says.

You weren't force-fed pictures of yourself?

49

I don't think there were many.

Come on.

I didn't have much of a relationship with my parents—don't have.

Gabe lights up and there's just the sound of traffic for a while. Bottles being unloaded onto the sidewalk below.

Is that something which bothers you? she then asks. About your parents?

Not really, he says. We don't have much in common.

It's never occurred to her to think of her parents as people with whom she may or may not have something in common.

They were young when they had me, he goes on, grew up with me in a way. My dad fixed up cars for a living and my mum stayed at home. I think they found my interest in music quite hard to understand.

He takes a breath then hesitates, like he's not going to say what he then goes on to say, which is that his uncle lived with them for most of his childhood. His dad's brother. Made home a pretty violent place to be.

He swings around and she tries her best not to look at his dick, which is perfect, like a drawing of a dick, while he's telling her that's why he got out early, moved across the country after he quit London.

Had to hustle for a while, he says, when I got to New York. Played on the subway, did some life modelling, stuff like that.

He seems very far away while he's saying these things, like a character on a window seat in a play.

It's an old story anyway, he concludes. Not current.

Radical, this idea. The past as a thing which expires.

What about that print, anyway? he then asks.

Which one?

With the cuts.

The Fontana, he means, just inside Anna's front door. Three vertical slashes cut into a cobalt-blue canvas.

A she? he asks.

A he—it's one of my favourites.

This is true, as it happens. Wild to find it at Anna's, though strangely muzzled in 2D. It's one of his *Tagli*, she explains. Which means slashes. They came after his *Buchi*, which means holes. The hole was his big discovery—the idea was to connect the viewer with the space behind the canvas, which he meant as a kind of infinity.

Can't you just see a bit of room, or wall, through the holes?

No, they're covered with this black mesh which swallows you into nowhere. No one knows how he makes the slashes either. I found a documentary online, where he lets them film right up to the cut, then has them come back in two hours. Could be the work of a second, or something much more involved.

I like that.

Right. It's objectively beautiful, I think, but it's the pressure release for me, more than anything. That puncturing. I saw a room full of *Tagli* at the Tate when I was a teenager and for ages had this recurring dream of the other side of the canvas—knives sticking through.

You're a therapist's dream, Gabe says, walking back to the bed.

It wasn't a violent thing, to be honest.

As I said . . .

She did try therapy, about a year after she moved to New York. Told her friend Sally she found sex painful a lot of the time, pleasurable, still, but also uncomfortable. Sally said it was typically British and repressed to live like that and sent her to see a woman on Tenth Street. She went, a few times, but the woman, who was obsessed with her childhood, found her so darkness-free she was forced to latch on to the time her uncle sat on her bed for what felt like an uncomfortably long time, when she was about seven. How she'd just made herself go to sleep and hadn't been aware of him leaving. That was the whole memory. She'd really had to search for it and there was nothing in it, but she'd sat with this woman for an hour, then two more after that, paying her to connect it to her sex life over two decades later. She doesn't share this with Gabe, but they briefly discuss the idea of therapy, and he says he doesn't believe in using the past to explain or try to fix the present—doesn't think it can—then starts to kiss the round part of her stomach. She agrees, which is easy to do, given she has no past, just an uncomfortable moment, one evening, as a child, being loved too much by a relative.

No dimension, no footnotes at all.

Six

At the weekend, she takes the High Line to the theatre.

Still in hibernation, last time she came up; tiny witch hazel blooms along the section at Little West Twelfth, here and there a crocus between tracks. All heady, honey garlic now, while further up, wind-bent grass makes a mad sky-prairie over Washington. As she takes these things in, she's also shaping them into the thing she'll describe later, in the line for the theatre. Each one a proof point in a case she's building, for what? She's editing, too, as she observes, the girl on the bench in front of her now, for example, whose face reflects back her own expression, most likely, and threatens to expose this moment as one of lemming-like conformity. Out walking the High Line, like someone let off the cruise ship.

Shizophragma, she stoops to read, and wonders what Gabe had meant by, 'stuff like that', talking about how he kept himself afloat when he first moved to the city.

Life modelling and, 'stuff like that', he'd said, perfect pink mound of dick in his lap.

Chokeberry, Chokecherry, Narcissus Hawera.

At Twentieth, she takes the stairs down to sidewalk level. The theatre's on Twenty-Sixth but she prefers to cross here, or at Twenty-First, for those blocks between Tenth and Ninth, which are the kind of New York City blocks you can only laugh about, or sing about, or cry about how you can never quite get at them, even as you're walking down them. This giddy red-brown townhouse medley grinds to a halt at Rite Aid, where she stops now, for Goobers. Totally bogus, as it happens—a Goober. Just a chocolate-coated peanut. Word feels good in the mouth, though. Looks good on the box. Box feels good in the hand.

One communal horn, it sounds like, turning onto Eighth Avenue, and a line already snaking around the side of Gristedes as she comes up on Twenty-Sixth. There's improv here every night of the week, but *Assscat*'s the big draw. A Sunday show where the audience suggests a word, which inspires a monologue, which inspires a series of improvised sketches. The name *Assscat* comes from one of the troupe's early shows back in Chicago, which bombed so hard it got to a point where one of them was stranded alone on stage in an imagined igloo and no one had it in them to join him. After a while one of them started to release this word-noise into the silence . . . *assscat* . . . others joining in from the wings, or wherever, just to be doing something, anything, chanting it together, inflating its strangeness like some kind of verbal life raft. Except there was no saving anyone as the worst had already happened.

She showed up the first time because of what this story did to her brain, then kept going due to a morbid fascination with the kind of person who'd put themselves in a situation like that, week after week. It's a sort of social experiment, half watching the show, half observing the performers as a species, trying to grasp the fundamental difference between herself and someone who'd risk being igloo guy, or girl. Sally started coming, a few months in. Her idea of a nightmare, an improv person, improv people, but the self-harm component appealed—Dylan's *British pain* watching the thing play out. After this, Addie joined, because she and Sally were going, then Javi and Clark because Sally brings coke. Once a month, they do this. *Assscat* then Red Cat, same table for years now, like the cast of some limping sitcom. A few lines with their crispy squid.

She can see Addie now, near the back of the standby line. Black, probably cashmere, sweater, artfully half-tucked into black cropped pants. Black ankle boots. Something fitted with something oversized, her go-to. A drop-shouldered energy that's usually at odds with her body language, on the phone now, for example, one arm gesturing, wrapping up a call. Her Hindi name, Aadya, means 'first', which is the vision her grandparents had for their family, she says, when they moved to the States from Bombay. It also speaks to something in Addie that's motivating and exhausting in equal measure.

She pulls Dylan in for a hug, debriefs on her week, then asks whether she saw the super blood moon last night, which was also a blue moon, or whatever, which is apparently a once-in-a-generation thing. Or a decade. Definitely rare.

Are you sure it was last night?

Yes. I was on the red-eye, so missed it—that's also why I look like shit.

She does not look like shit.

I'm pretty sure I'd have seen it, Dylan says.

She and Gabe had been out on the fire escape again, for at least an hour. So absorbed by one another that they hadn't noticed what was going on above them? A super blue, blood moon, or whatever.

Addie checks her phone.

Wait, you're right, it hasn't happened yet.

Oh. Okay.

Addie leans out and looks down the line in both directions.

Sally can't make it, she says. Had to head upstate early.

The boys already cancelled during the week, so it'll just be the two of them. Precarious, she senses, instinctively; Addie unusually taut and sudden, now swapping her phone for a pot of Carmex, making a tight fist around it.

You know I bumped into Matt at Oakland, she says.

Yeah, he mentioned.

He's got a pretty great set-up over there.

It definitely suits him.

When were you last over, anyway?

He made me go for Valentine's Day. Which he knows I hate energetically.

You're not at all tempted?

By what?

To move West.

No.

Really not?

Really not. If anyone's moving, it's Matt—back to New York.

So someone is moving?

No one is moving. Anyway, I'm pretty sure we're too old to be talking about boys in line for improv.

Fine, says Addie. Is egg freezing a more age-appropriate conversation? Because I'm doing mine.

Okay, that sounds . . . Really?

Addie explains the procedure, which sounds invasive.

It's fairly routine, she adds. They've even started pushing it as a graduation present.

Which isn't at all fucked up.

Right. Anyway, the company healthcare covers it, which I grant is creepy, and a whole other thing, but it seems crazy not to take advantage. Your eggs are pretty much shot by the time you hit thirty-eight, which is only a few years away.

I'm done in a week, then?

Wait, no—just for freezing, you know what I mean . . . they say to do it before then.

Dylan's always assumed she'll have kids, but in a way that requires no obvious intervention on her part. She'll have them at some point, is the idea, when things have fallen into place. What things, exactly, and on what timeline, is unclear, but she's never had any real sense a door might be closing soon, or at all. It's bizarre to hear Addie talk about intervening, thinking she has to, not just because she's several years younger, but because it's impossible not to imagine the inside of her body as well put together as the outside. Womb, like a flawless classic six. Highly strung little embryo propped among Bergdorf throw cushions.

Dude, come *on* . . .

Someone has stepped out of line to gesture at a guy crouching behind the Citi bikes, apparently taking a shit.

Poop guy holds up a hand like, just wrapping up, then buttons his pants, walks on.

What does it cost anyway? Dylan asks.

It varies. Somewhere between ten and fifteen thousand. More if I do a second round.

Christ, doesn't that seem immoral?

Says the ad executive.

Ex, actually, she says.

Wait, what?

She'd not meant to share this yet, with anyone, definitely not Addie, but she's started now, so fills her in on everything but Gabe.

So you just walked out?

Right.

During an all-agency meeting.

A talk, but yes.

Then how did you actually resign?

By email—and I know what you're going to say.

Addie pauses for a moment, as though she might not say the predictable thing, before then saying the predictable thing.

You will be, though. Fucked for a reference.

Frankly, it helps to think I'm burning that bridge.

Okay.

I mean, there's something a bit non-committal about paving your way back into the thing you're trying to leave, while you're leaving it.

The lid's off the Carmex now, Addie rubbing at it like she's trying to get it off.

And you'll be paying rent how?

She explains about the housesit, the sublet money.

There's some pension, too—which I'm not touching yet.

And what does Matt think?

I haven't told him yet.

You're kidding.

It hasn't got much to do with him.

How can you say that?

It's my career, Dylan continues. And it's only been three weeks . . . less than. He's flying over next weekend anyway, so we'll speak then.

Three weeks?

Addie begins to grope in her bag, as though for some reason this is the last straw.

Jesus, Addie.

It's just weird you haven't told him yet.

Addie opens a Mountain Dew, makes a tiny 'o' with her mouth, and takes an impossibly intense sip. The 'o' remains as she screws the cap back on. Some piece of debris from Dylan's decision-making inexplicably lodged there, causing this rictus.

It's not the most important thing, says Dylan.

And what is? I mean, do you even have a sense of where this has come from?

I can't believe you're asking me that. We hate our jobs. It's ninety per cent of what we talk about. When you were staying at my place, you actually used to say the words every morning, going down the stoop—I hate my job, I hate my job. You know you were saying it out loud, right?

Addie makes a face like she's betraying her trust with an observation like this.

That was when I was at the agency.

The consultancy is worse . . . What's that brief you asked me to look at last week?

She wakes her phone.

I know the one you mean, says Addie. You can put that down. Here it is:

How can a popular brand of paper plate join the conversation about trans awareness without alienating its core market in the Midwest?

Yeah, well, you weren't exactly helpful.

I mean fuck, Addie, you're Columbia Cum Kappa Laude, or whatever.

You don't have to shit on the rest of us just because you're five minutes into enlightenment.

That's not what I'm doing.

I just don't want you to screw yourself.

That's kind, she says, but you seem to need me to feel that I have.

Addie returns the Mountain Dew to her bag, so she can use both hands to paint a picture of support given and received, going way back into the archives. Her eyes broaden, then narrow, as she does this, and it occurs to Dylan, not for the first time, how fucked up female friendship can be. Its celebrated superpowers, at their worst, just another way to identify yourself as defective in human relationships. That unwritten contract to unfold energies towards one another, a source of intimacy, sure, but also something much more insidious, some kind of shared biography you're meant to get behind, that you have no control over, that lives inside the tiny 'o'. She'd like to raise these things with Addie, then, calmly, as two progressive women, draft a new kind of contract together.

You act like I'm trying to confuse you, she says instead.

What's that supposed to mean?

Like my life decisions are part of some intricate plot to throw you off your game.

So you want platitudes?

Honestly, Addie, I don't want anything from you.

Addie becomes completely still.

Need anything from you, Dylan says. You know what I mean.

The ushers, who've been making a headcount, now stop a few feet away and turn back.

You know what I meant, says Dylan.

Sure.

Addie looks at her watch, then back at the theatre.

I'm going to see what's up.

Dylan watches her start down the sidewalk, unhandled *FT* poking from her bag, like a pretty, pink stick of executive rock, and for a moment her resentment is dwarfed by a wave of fondness that is wholly non-contractual. Then she's pissed again, agitated by the fact of this line, the absurdity of her in it, of willing waiting heads wound around New York City blocks. The person right behind her is only now asking what this line is for— something good, must be—as the low light shrinks to a wedge on the side of Gristedes.

Addie reappears, shrugging.

She'd been lukewarm about showing up but now feels like she desperately needs the catharsis of maybe igloo-gate to paper over the thinness of things. She could have left earlier, but it's that time of year when bright afternoons are back. Make you think you've got time to spare.

Seven

Thursday in Coney.

Skeletons of Cyclone and Wonder Wheel against so much open sky.

To the right, Luna Park, flat, like a postcard.

To the left, the Atlantic, swaying.

Up ahead, empty boardwalk, a kid chasing gulls.

Gabe is eating a hot dog, his second, and she asks if he can see the same cloud shapes she's seeing—splayed cartoon baby, hooked wisdom tooth, almost-asterisk or fraying star. No, he says, then asks how many spokes, arms, whatever, an asterisk is meant to have, officially.

They teach you that at Oxford?

They do not, she says, amused he's looked her up.

He shrugs.

Looks more like a hubcap anyway.

His footsteps sound certain on the boardwalk, like a mallet knocking in pegs. Every now and then he reaches over and touches her body somewhere surprising; just below her collar, for example, running his fingers over the bumps on her spine.

He stops twice to feed her the thing he's eating.

The second time, adds finger.

After Coney, they take Beach Channel Drive in his old Charger, olive green, front seat like a booth at a diner. They pull up at a remote spot, where he then stands in front of a faded No Swimming sign and strips down to white underpants. The kind you get in a three-pack at Target.

Won't the water be insane? she says.

He shakes his arms out.

Brisk, he says, and she thinks how you don't hear brisk much. Brisk walk, brisk breeze, brisk tone . . .

Maybe you do hear brisk.

Now he asks if she'll join him. He has mistaken her for someone who does things. Someone who is free, not free-curious. She'd like to be the first one in, to want to be. As a kid, she'd sit in the sea for hours, pale skin cycling through purple, orange, blue, but somewhere in her twenties her body stopped complying. Cold too much of a shock to the system. Now she rolls up her jeans and follows him ankle-deep, pretending she'd join him if she had a swimsuit. The same way she'd feigned disappointment when they found out the rollercoaster was closed, weekends only until Memorial Day. Maybe he doesn't see through her, maybe he does. Maybe it makes no difference at all to him what she's like.

Gabe carries on up to his waist. He has his back to her now, and it occurs to her she can't fill in his face. When he glances back, it seems obvious again, like of course that's his face, then he's under a wave and she can't see him at all. He swims further out, then stops and bobs for a while, like a flesh-coloured buoy. On his way back in, he walks as soon as he can stand, so that for a while only the broad part of him is showing above the water, hair slicked to his chest. The boy part then follows, skinny legs shaking involuntarily. She can see his dick though his wet underpants—short, thick, off to the left—imagines how it would feel in her mouth, how he'd react if she went down on him right now. Would he think of her differently? What does he think of her now?

He towels off, pulls on a sweater, says they should dig a hole. This is unexpected.

At some point she'd said she likes unseasonal beach. That's why Coney, he explained in the car. What she likes is the way everything feels at a distance, the usual beach things out of reach, packed away. She hadn't explained this, and now he's handing her a spade. He's brought two. She helps for a while, gesturally, then sits on her jacket and pulls a book from her bag. *The Artist's Way*. Recommended by a friend as a tool for unblocking creativity. *The Way to Art* is the title they'd actually given, which is more honest about the art being over there, usually, while you are over here. It's divided into thirteen weeks, each with its own chapter, then various tasks, all of them mortifying. Also, daily freewriting, which seems too obvious a contradiction to attempt. This is a library copy, multiple bookmarks abandoned at different stages, like corpses on Everest.

Halfway through Chapter Four: *Recovering a Sense of Integrity*, she becomes acutely aware of the cold breeze on her cheek, hard sand beneath her feet, the sound of its surface being broken, broken again by Gabe's shovel, off to her right, so that for a split second she can feel herself at the edge of a place from which she might either zoom out and see the moment as a kind of whole or disappear into the flesh of it. Even in the forming of this thought she's aware she's chosen seeing. How then to be always seeing, and not seeing through?

She puts all three bookmarks in the current page and joins Gabe, now waist deep, sleeves rolled to his elbows. His arms are pale like hers, but you can tell he'll tan in the summer, which she will not. She climbs onto a nearby crop of rocks and sits. On the other side, there are crab carcasses for at least twenty feet.

That's macabre, she says.

Gabe looks up from his hole.

What?

The crabs.

You've not seen that before?

Never. What's killed them?

Who knows.

Gabe sticks his spade into a large pile of sand.

Will you get in?

Into what?

The hole.

Yeah, no thanks.

Let me bury you.

In this outfit?

Maybe this will work again.

Let me, he says, then pulls himself up and walks over to the

66

car. He comes back with a large waterproof, which hits just below her knees.

Come on, just a bit.

You want to bury me a bit?

It's childish and the sand will be a nightmare, but she finds she wants to do what he wants, likes him telling her what that is, so she lets him bury her. The hole is deep, for this game, which of course she's played before, but she lies there, smiling, waiting for him to notice her, taken up, as he now is, with the business of shovelling. He keeps going until she's unable to crack the sand with her feet, or by moving her chest, which is when she asks him to stop.

Come on, he says.

Please stop.

He continues, legs either side of her.

Now, she says.

He pauses.

Please.

Killjoy.

He climbs out and is immediately invisible. He may not have gone far, but the sides of the hole are too high to see over, and she is not having fun. This is not a fun game. What does she even know about this guy? She tries to relax her body. Notices then how the sea sounds lower below ground, and nearer, as if the next wave might be the one to cover her face.

I'd like to get out of here, she says.

Nothing.

She calls his name then, which feels strange in her mouth, not quite attached to him yet—Gabe. Too neat for the idea of him.

The smell of food arrives before his face, leaning over the edge of the hole, taking a bite out of the thick deli sandwich he must have brought with him. He pauses for a moment, to swallow, then re-wraps his sub, jumps in and digs. As soon as she feels the sand begin to give, she sits up. With his help, the rest of her follows.

On the way back to Manhattan, they do not discuss the hole. They are not talking at all. Perhaps talking is over. She feels at once deserving of an apology but also somehow responsible for the atmosphere in the car. Whenever Gabe looks over at her, she looks right back, thinking maybe she should turn away more. Now, specifically, but also in general.

She opens her phone, searches, scrolls.

It's just exoskeleton, she says—the crabs. Not carcasses. They have to moult to grow, which is also usually when they mate.

Okay, says Gabe.

It's called undressing.

Huh.

She reads:

Crabs must shed their exoskeleton in order to grow. Only in this post-moulting state, can the female reproduce. Once a chemical connection has been made, the male will gather her into a pre-mating 'hug'. The female succumbs only when the male has proven his strength and therefore suitability as a mate. The embrace will usually continue for several days, sometimes more than a week, until the female moults and copulation occurs. After this

the male will hold the female until her shell hardens, then leave her to seek
a new partner. The female will reproduce alone, at a later date.

Gabe grins and pats the seat beside him.

She's inclined to ask for her apology, but moves closer instead. He slides his right hand off the wheel, slips it around her waist, then pinches the flesh just above her jeans.

It says hug not pinch.

You're sure about that?

Also, that's not a part of the body to go after.

This little snack? he says, and pinches again.

She likes snack, likes that Gabe's into this part of her, which is almost the same as liking it herself.

In the bathroom she sucks his fingers, then his dick.

They don't make it into the shower because they're lying on his bathmat and he's already asking if she wants him to fuck her without a condom. She says that she does. He asks again, closer to her ear now, already inside her.

Yes, she says—keeps on saying.

Afterwards:

Kate's flying in later, he explains, or he'd ask her to stick around. Also, would she mind wearing stockings for him some time?

Flesh-coloured, he says. I like the old kind.

Eight

Matt's voicemails go like this:

He's shown up early to surprise her.

He's at her work but the guy at the front desk says it's not actually—her work.

Should he wait?

He'll wait.

He's outside her apartment, but there's a sticker over her buzzer, some guy called Zeb? This makes no sense.

He's going to wait.

Should he?

Her super is beside him now, saying, I do not know where is Dylan, then Dylan is Airbnb, then here is something not legal.

He should say nothing, right?

Sally is not picking up. Addie is not picking up. Clark and Javi are not picking up, so he's going to wait on her stoop . . . Zeb's stoop . . . seriously, what the fuck?

The last message was an hour ago and what the fuck is a relief when it comes, as everything else is said in the measured tone of someone who does not experience normal human emotions. After Matt's voicemails, there's a voicemail from Addie saying she has a voicemail from Matt and it's pretty fucked up she hasn't spoken to him yet, not just because he's got a whole trip planned for this weekend. Everyone's coming.

She'd planned exactly how to catch Matt up, in a way guaranteed to win his support and make him feel unreasonable for questioning her motives in any way. She's run through both sides of the conversation multiple times, so that telling him was going to be like revisiting something previously discussed, which she knows turns out fine. She could have avoided the current situation, of course, by telling him earlier, about work at least. Why hadn't she? She'd wanted a secret, perhaps, but it's no longer the main secret. There are multiple layers of secret, and this one is somewhere near the top, barely relevant.

She texts Matt saying she can't speak now, but to please meet her at the Bowery Hotel. There's a simple explanation and she's sorry.

She'd pictured herself in the corner of that high-backed sofa, under the palm by the lobby fireplace. The fire would be going, though it's basically May, and Matt would find her there, working on a cocktail. He would sit down beside her and make the face he makes when he's expecting her to speak first. She'd take one more sip—her ice cubes would seem loud when she did this—then they'd get into it.

This is not what happens, as that sofa is occupied. Also, the one opposite. As a result, they're sitting at the dark bar near the elevators, on the middle two stools in a row of eight, all full. The stools are comically high and so close together that you either have to face the bar straight-on or intermingle legs. She and Matt have gone for intermingle legs, rather than sideways conversation. The sheer scale of him forces her knees naturally upward, between his, which is probably more intimacy than he's happy with, in the circumstances. He has that flushed outward-bound look he gets when he's frustrated, like he's just finished a hike. So far, he's said hello and ordered a drink.

You've changed your hair, he says.

Job, he means. Address.

Yes.

What's it for?

It's a haircut, Matt. It's not a big deal.

It had been, naturally. She went to a place on Avenue A, where they mocked her for asking for a few inches off, after a long discussion, so she'd said fine, do what you like. It could have been worse, but the length of the bangs sends out the wrong message about her decision to do something creative, which she does mean and is not saying just to say. Matt's hair is the same. Thick, just-out-of-bed energy on top, short at the back, almost buzzcut, so she can feel the shape of his skull when she's lying next to him, reach out with both hands and find out that small roundness where neck ends and skull begins. Knowing him, somehow, in this.

Ideally he can lift me above his head, she'll usually say, when asked about her type—not completely joking. Some painfully regressive notion about feeling feminine or protected, Sally seems to think, and yes, maybe, to both of those things. Like a fern at the foot of a redwood with Matt, it's true. But a brilliant green. Lush and complex, there. In constant motion against his solid brown. He is crisp and pressed-looking tonight, which means that, despite the afternoon he's had, he's still dressed up to meet her; found some café restroom and changed from flight clothes into going-out clothes. Matt is not getting a fair shake. This is clear, though feels separate from her somehow. Just as she is beginning to feel separate from herself. Further and further away from her choices, which seem to have less and less to do with things she's choosing. She's just let Gabe fuck her without a condom, for example. So there's that.

She takes Matt's hand and explains, everything but Gabe. It all sounds remarkably unimportant said in one go. He says she should have told him, that it's strange she didn't, but overall his reaction is measured and rational, which sidesteps the drama she'd anticipated in a way that points the spotlight very clearly ahead, to what comes next. The idea of anything coming next makes her want to slide off the stool onto the floor and just lie there, but Matt's still talking, asking how long the housesit will be. Five months, she tells him, though it's only three. And yes, she has health insurance, for now.

When he asks about her plans to support herself, she reminds him about her green card, then savings, though these are minimal, and says that writing, ideally, is the plan. She feels like a circus bear when she says this, not just because no one lives off writing, but because there's no pen moving across paper, words on a screen, anything happening, at all, in any format.

Do you think that might be too much pressure to put on it? he asks. The writing, I mean.

You think I'm insane.

No. You're obviously a writer. The way you look at stuff has always been—

He tips his glass, just slightly, as if to demonstrate something about perspective.

You'll be a great one.

But?

But nothing.

She can't seem to pick a fight. Matt is on board. Even at her worst, he's always credited her with a sort of high-functioning restlessness. Matt, who is that rare thing, which is happy at work. Kind as well as successful. There to fuck with every part of her world view. Maybe work has nothing to do with it and she is straightforwardly restless, Matt straightforwardly kind. Yet Matt is not easily summable up. Not just because she can never quite place an American—usually a turn-on—but because it took nearly six months of dating, for example, before she learned he'd lost a brother. Adam, he offered up, walking her home one night. Died second year of college. Death-in-bed syndrome, caused by night-time hypoglycaemia. They were close, only two years apart. Wherever Adam was, there was Matt, keeping an eye out. Same college, too, Matt making sure of this, doing his Masters just to stick around until Adam's graduation. Baffling how he'd handled the way things played out.

The Power Bar, she's always thought had something to do with Adam. When she got her last promotion, she bought herself the least offensive bag that would take a laptop, which had this weird side pocket that didn't fit a phone or water bottle and was basically pointless. First day in the new role, Matt slipped a Power Bar in there, which is not a thing she'd ever eat, nor would ever encounter, but fit perfectly in this space. Occasionally he'd switch it out, like one changes a bedsheet, but it was never absent—her hand routinely clamped around the pleasing rectangle of it on the 1 Train early morning, late at night. Matt put a ring in there once, just before he moved to San Francisco. She found him waiting down in the office lobby. Bad, that had been, all around. Too early, he'd agreed, instantly, apologising, saying something about the move, and no big deal, and seriously, forget about it for a while.

Now his flushed look is gone, and he waves over the bartender.

A gin and tonic is $16.

This is insane.

She orders a gin and tonic.

Another.

After two more, she's become fixated on the woman a few stools over, with arched black lines tattooed where her shaved eyebrows had been. So certain there should be no eyebrows, then that they should never leave her, express only surprise. Something profound in this, she's trying to land with Matt, as he picks up the check and walks her through the lobby.

Out on the sidewalk:

It's a small bar, he says.

What?

You were saying eyebrows a lot.

I was?

Kind of aggressively.

She laughs, then takes the hand he's offering.

It's noticeably warmer tonight, a feeling of May burgeoning as they turn onto Third Street, where there are sweatpants full of shit. The smell arrives first, hits the way shit hits, right at the back of the throat. Then the visual, which is an extreme shit situation. Two giant, curled deposits, like a pair of resting cobras. Exquisite poop symmetry laid into high-end grey marl—acne label bright white in the lamplight. Matt says he saw this on his way over, and seems pleased it's still doing its thing, which is to both surprise and confirm, for a person like Matt, something fundamental about the city. That only matching shit cobras in $300 sweatpants can deliver. Best not to question this philosophy, which most likely comes from the same place as Matt's other grand narratives, about her, for example—equally epic, and vague, and forgiving. Something to do with him not being able to place her in the same way she cannot place him? And the angle he was trying to find on that glass. Other things too. All of them saved in the cloud of Matt. Whole, functioning versions of selves that can be revisited at any time. She is relieved to be saved on Matt. Also, she is saved on Matt and cannot get out.

Just as they arrive at the red door, a cab pulls up beside them. Dylan, hi.

Kate steps out, with a small suitcase. She is so vivid conceptually, at this point, that the flesh edition is truly startling.

Welcome back, says Dylan.

Kate adjusts the handle on her bag.

You noticed I was gone?

No. Not really.

She pauses, tries again.

I mean, I bumped into Gabe, and he mentioned it. You know, that you were not here . . . on a work trip or something. So yeah.

Matt looks at her like she's about to say eyebrows again, then leans forward and introduces himself to Kate, first as her boyfriend, then by name.

Kate shakes his hand.

I'm downstairs. How come we've not seen you around?

Based in San Francisco.

Huh, she says, and makes a quick scan of him.

You guys should come over for drinks while you're here.

Before Dylan can enjoy the sound of Matt turning Kate down, he's giving her a hand with her bag and they're all headed up the stairs together. Kate asks about Matt's work, among other things, while Dylan tries to set a pace that won't allow for too much exposition. There's no sign of Gabe, thankfully, when they leave Kate at her door.

She seems nice, says Matt, meaning attractive, then after a quick tour of the apartment, he tells her to pack a bag. He has a surprise planned, and they leave in the morning. She arranges her face into shock, then delight, but both expressions feel exactly the same as the sexually knowing face she tried to make for Gabe when they first fucked.

Getting ready for bed:

Are you considering art as well? Matt says.

He's holding up her personality Venn diagram from the park.

78

The hand-drawn version—two sagging ovals, grim slit, like a sad vagina.

What's this meant to be?

She can't remember what each circle is meant to represent but has no trouble picturing how easily Matt would set about filling them in on her behalf. He would have fun doing this and it would be fun to read. The fun being had by all would be directly proportionate to the fun not being had by her, now, faced with this absurd diagram. And there's rage, suddenly, at all the ways she can imagine he might be right in his fillings in, at how hard she has worked to ensure this muscle is well developed in him. She, now and for ever, pre-filled as a result.

Fuck off, would you?

She snatches the paper from him, balls it into the trash, then goes back to reviewing the two fine lines that have started to appear on her upper lip, which are much more pronounced in Anna's bathroom light. They're the kind that smokers get, though she's never smoked, or had the pleasure of a cigarette, as she's never been able to inhale. She's bound to be one of those people who spend their lives with little-boy breasts and get breast cancer too. It seems obvious something of this kind is in store for her, and that it won't be the thing she thought to worry about. When Matt starts up about his latest project, she thinks of Gabe.

Of that massive sandwich for some reason.

Of the way he pinched her snack of flesh in the car.

Of the bathroom later.

Nine

The house is right on the beach.

Matt didn't say how he pulled it off, just that he's happy he managed to get everyone together for her birthday this year. Dylan doesn't like celebrating it, so they're doing a dinner tonight and not speaking of it tomorrow, which is the actual day. Sally's hustled her onto the deck with a bottle of champagne, probably meant for later, and two mugs. They've put sofa cushions on the sunbeds and are sitting cross-legged in the matching men's parkas they found in the entrance hall.

Sally balances her lit cigarette on a saucer, rolls up an over-sized sleeve and fills both mugs. Her hair, which is dark, thick, and naturally quite wild, has been blown into something other-worldly by the salt-sticky breeze. It suits her. The coat does too, like most things. She's one of the first people Dylan met in the city, the then girlfriend of one of her colleagues, she'd shown up at drinks one night, full-figured, mouthy, undeniable. Sick of her circle, she'd announced, quite early on, then Dylan made a joke that was only half a joke about the benefits of having no circle at all and after that Sally had taken her everywhere, as though they'd agreed on something fundamental about the city, or other people, or something else altogether. The closeness stuck, despite Sally's thing for people churn, and the fact she's been out of the city for the last six months, upstate with her woodworker boyfriend—focusing on personal projects, she says, which could mean anything.

Let's go, then.

Let's go what?

Your message, Sally says. You've got something to tell me.

She'd planned to tell her about Gabe, but now they're all together, fridge full of booze, Matt just the other side of the glass door, she's not sure.

It's nothing, she says, just the work thing.

Oh.

Sally lies back.

That's great, though. Way overdue.

Ideally the conversation would end here.

So now what?

The point was to write. Is to write.

The point of what?

Of now.

She should have said personal projects.

It's not a long-term plan, she adds.

Well, get on with it, and maybe you'll stumble into a plan.

It's the right advice, but she hasn't been around Sally for a while and wasn't prepared for such a straightforward response.

I just feel sad, she says, not expecting to say these words, definitely not now, but also not surprised to hear them.

Well shit.

Sally slides the bottle across the low plastic table.

I know. I'm sorry. I don't know why I just said that.

They lie back together.

The beach is windswept and empty, save for the lone runner who passed them on their way out of the house, shrunk to a dot now against the bruised grey-blue. The image of Gabe, then, wading into the water at Coney. The way she couldn't picture his face when it was turned from her. She can picture it now, quite clearly, but something about his physical presence had made him harder to remember.

Sally asks what she's doing about rent and she fills her in on the housesit. They briefly discuss the piece of art over Anna's toilet, then Sally says how much she's enjoying living in a barn.

Not hating the city either, she adds.

Now you're not in it?

Sally shrugs, wipes her sunglasses.

Addie said something similar on the way over, Dylan continues. How important it is to get out of the city, how necessary, as though there's some hidden profundity in a Hamptons weekend. Matt nodding up front, like her friendly getaway driver. Now we're here I bet you neither of them gets past the deck.

We haven't made it past the deck.

That's not the point.

Of now?

You're actually hilarious, says Dylan, zipping her jacket. March weather, this feels like, not May.

Sally tucks her feet under a cushion.

So, who's in your place while you're housesitting?

Airbnb.

My friend Irene is screwing her Airbnb guy. She basically shows up at the apartment she can no longer afford, sleeps with him, then has to wait to be asked to stay.

That's nice.

She's finding the whole thing a bit of a mindfuck, apparently. Something to do with the fact there's money changing hands.

She might have a point.

Sex and a stipend, what's not to love? And she knows where to find shit in the morning.

When she's invited to stay.

Right.

Sally pulls on her last inch of cigarette, a habit that makes it look like she's trying to smoke her fingers.

So, when do I get to read some of your stuff anyway?

I have a half thing, says Dylan—half a thing.

Which is it?

Half a thing.

Okay.

Apparently, I'm not of the literary moment.

Okay.

Sally has either lost interest or is trying to get her to reveal herself in some way.

That was my last feedback.

84

On what?

Just a piece of flash fiction.

What needs to happen, Sally asks, in a piece of flash fiction, to make it flash fiction?

Every time she says flash fiction it sounds more like the punchline to a joke, something Dylan's invented to hide the fact she's unable to manage something more substantial on the page. The last thing she had published was back in London, two short stories just before she left, but she's failed to build on this momentum in New York. For some reason only able to deal in fragments.

Decent flash fiction, Sally clarifies—the kind that makes it into the tiny cannon.

She makes herself laugh with this question.

Dylan closes her eyes.

Anyway, you're good at little moves, Sally adds. You know, flipping something or coming at it weirdly.

Trickster, Sally means. Word clown. Impressive how casually she's managing to nail her shortcomings.

It's a novel I'm working on, she says.

So, you identify as novel. Did the feedback say what moment you are of?

Not so much.

She thought about this when she got the rejection; not what moment she might belong to, but what the Literary Moment might be, if there is one, and she is not inside it. Some moment writers share together, that's not a part of the other moment—the clock one—split in their being, as they are anyway, in one place writing, but also in the elsewhere they're creating. Regardless, it's no surprise to hear she's out of step, with the moment, herself, whatever.

The good news is nobody's watching, says Sally.

Nice.

I mean that in the best possible way, like a, Let it set you free, kind of way.

The conservatory door slides open, and Matt's head appears, asking whether they need anything from town.

They do not.

The door slides closed.

Sally slips the cellophane from a fresh pack of Newports.

I have to ask, she says—

It's going to be something about Matt.

Does Matt actually get you off?

She points her cigarette at the door, as though it somehow speaks to Matt's questionable sexual charisma. Strong, white . . . menthol?

Do you have to ask?

I mean he's hard not to like, Sally continues.

And?

It makes me suspicious.

Which probably says more about you than Matt.

It's unclear whether she's defending Matt because she means to or because she's been caught off-guard by the sex challenge, which is a new one. The niceness thing comes up a lot, especially with Sally. The truth is, he can get her off, but usually needs help, which begs the question does he actually need to be there for it to happen.

I mean, how does it even work with him in San Francisco?

Same way any long-distance relationship works.

They don't, in my experience.

You'd end things with Dan if he moved West?

Supplement, maybe.

As in?

Find something on the East Coast as well. But you'd need someone who has their own thing going on too, so there's no drama down the road.

Sally puts her hand to her temple, as though filtering candidates. The ring on her middle finger overlaps in chunky, gold sections, like mini armour or some kind of futuristic insect.

I don't see the point in staying in something that doesn't make you happy, Dylan says. Or in having something on the side where neither of you are invested.

It seems disingenuous to say this, is disingenuous, but it's also how she feels, which is clearly problematic, or what she thinks, despite the way she's behaving. Regardless, it's hard to resist the fact Sally's making it possible to have the conversation she'd wanted, some of it at least, with nothing at stake.

You haven't thought about it? Sally asks.

No. I don't know . . . maybe.

If you were a guy, you'd absolutely have thought about it.

Sally goes on to say she shouldn't confuse sex with what makes her happy or assume both things have to come from the same relationship, any relationship.

Matt is painfully, pathetically in love with you, she says, and it's nice, I guess, if that's your thing, but there's no way you can

87

cater to all of his needs either, and if he thinks you can then you two have bigger problems than whether or not he gets you off.

I said he did.

You didn't, actually.

Sally slides her lighter onto the table and begins to drum her fingers. She's been quitting since before they met, and this pause between cigarettes represents major progress.

You know, when I moved in with Dan, I was still seeing a girl in the city. For a while, actually, someone from work.

This is news to Dylan, who is yet to meet Dan and has the sudden sense of Sally's life lived as some kind of covert operation.

Perfect tits, she adds—small, round.

Did Dan know?

About her? No.

That you were into girls.

He asked pretty early on.

And?

Non-issue. He seemed to need language, though.

How do you mean?

So you're queer? he tried, which I'm not mad about. The word, I mean, as a noun, lazily conflated with sexuality. As a behaviour absolutely. Given the alternative, who wouldn't want to live queerly—sexually, socially, professionally . . . ?

The soup of being, Dylan says, thinking how professionally queer is a pleasing take on her current situation.

Sally lights up.

I love that.

Maggie Nelson, Dylan says.

So good. I masturbated to *The Argonauts*, furiously, in the first term of my MBA. That section about claiming your desires. Fuck.

Sally takes a long drag then leans back, top lip smudged, armour-ring hand hanging over the edge of her sunbed, like some kind of *Fight Club* mermaid.

Anyway, I don't know who Dan's been with, might still be seeing. That's his business. Right now, we're having a good time and I'm not actively looking for anything else, but that might change.

A lone gull wheels across the beach, swoops to collect something invisible from the sand, soars back upwards.

Dylan rolls onto her side.

The girl I'm housesitting for is stockpiling condoms in the most intense way.

How do you know?

It's like some kind of dirty tombola in her vanity. Jumbo tubes of lube in a sea of condoms. I mean, how much casual sex would you need to be having?

A teat, Sally says.

Sorry?

Of condoms. Wait—a sheath.

They're quiet for a while, then:

A jerk.

A spooge.

A coitus, they settle on.

The same gull, or a different gull, lands near the decking and noses the sand.

A rash of cunts, Sally then says.

A ravish, says Dylan. No, a *lavish*.

A lavish of cunts.

Sally swings around, as though her threshold for engagement has finally been met. Even smudged, her lips are sensuous, certain, the kind which make you think about kissing, with them, in Dylan's case, as their owner. How would it feel to kiss Gabe with Sally's lips? Different or the same? She has no clear memory of kissing Gabe with her own lips. This has happened, of course, many times, but there's an atomising sensation which accompanies all physical contact with him that makes it hard to remember particulars.

The conservatory door slides open again and Addie steps out wearing a large, wrap-around apron. Whatever's stuffed into its front pocket gives her the look of early pregnancy.

What are you guys up to?

Sea air, says Dylan.

Sally releases a thin column of smoke, blows it sideways.

Nice, says Addie. Also, we're actually missing some sofa cushions inside.

Something in this statement makes Dylan feel violent.

It's actually.

We're actually missing some cushions.

Yeah, she says. We couldn't find the sunbed ones.

Addie rests a hand on the back of Sally's lounger.

Probably best not to have white ones out here, she says, attempting a look of complicity, like she's been sent out, by herself, against her will.

Sally stands.

Who'd rent a beach house where everything's white?

Matt, evidently, says Dylan.

Asshole, Sally says, then pulls Addie into a bear hug.

Only in moments like these can she imagine Addie and Sally as kids, living on the same street, problematic mothers close friends. Joint family vacations, the whole thing, apparently, until they left for college on opposite sides of the country—Sally two years ahead. Pure chance they both landed in New York.

Actually, we found it together, says Addie.

She frees herself from Sally, then hands her a cushion.

Anyway, Javi and Clark just arrived.

Dylan grabs a cushion and follows them inside, where Javi and Clark are sitting on the sofa they didn't strip. This is also white and backs onto a white, open-plan kitchen. It's supposed to seat four but is so overloaded with nautically themed cushions—anchor, crab, Viking longboat?—that there's barely room for the two of them. Gabi is playing at their feet with the decorative wicker ball she's picked out of the ceramic bowl on the coffee table. She's just turned three, their surrogate daughter via an egg from New Jersey, Javi-or-Clark sperm, and a womb in Nevada. Addie has already identified her as a deposit liability and is crouched beside her, engaging her in a brief game which involves returning the wicker ball to its bowl and moving the bowl out of reach.

You two look impressively nautical, says Clark. What's a sailery, anyway?

He's looking at their parkas. *Hamptons Sailery* embroidered onto their matching breast pockets.

Fuck knows, says Sally. I'm pretty sure these aren't the kind that keep the fish out.

Javi looks at Sally like can we not curse in front of the kid and Clark looks at Dylan like how long have you guys been drinking?

Sally heads for the fridge, while Addie turns her attention from Gabi to Matt, just back from the fishmonger. Ruddy-faced and wholesome-looking in the jacket he did not forget to bring. She joins him in the kitchen—newspaper needs to be damp, not wet, Matty . . . we'll use the same box, bottom of the fridge. No one calls him Matty, but Addie likes giving instructions and Matt likes knowing what is expected of him, so this must be a rewarding experience for both of them. They've known each other since college and Clark says they dated briefly. It was Clark who introduced Matt to Dylan.

Sally reappears, stepping over Gabi.

Mind the child, says Clark.

You know how I feel about babies, she says, and hands him two glasses.

Do you guys ever freak out it's a girl? I can't think of two people who know less about girls.

You'll be a great parent too someday, says Javi.

You know what I mean.

Javi then makes a face like, yes, he does, and that's why he finds it offensive. He's a successful non-fiction writer—cultural criticism, mostly—from Mexico, via Princeton and Harvard, and recent recipient of a prestigious no-strings grant meant to allow his giant brain to roam freely. He picks his battles when it comes to Sally, tends to underestimate her, which usually results in her mouthing off. He has the opposite effect on Dylan, who he's decided is a fellow intellectual, and therefore either becomes mute under the weight of his expectation or does that British thing of undermining everything she's about to say . . . of course I'm clueless, must sound ridiculous, haven't read the whole Constitution. He's giving her that look of expectation now, as he says his happy not-birthdays and asks what freedom feels like. The question is throwaway, but she can feel herself reconfiguring, preparing to persuade him of something as yet unclear. The truth is freedom doesn't feel like anything at all. Or she's forgotten to feel it, how to feel altogether, or at least how to appropriately match feelings with stimulus. Like the pre-emptive guilt she was feeling about Matt that should have come a few weeks ago and by now have matured to fully-fledged guilt. Or how watching Addie and Matt—their creepy domestic harmony—she's thinking only about Gabe and Kate. Imagining them in their own white kitchen on, say, a Tuesday night. Do they cook together? What do they eat? What do they talk about? Themselves or other people? Or not about people at all, just about things? If so, what things? Does Gabe find Kate intelligent? He doesn't know she's intelligent yet, she can sense this, so could well have missed it in his wife.

His wife.

She tries to feel the weight of this properly, but her next thought is that if Sally's right and she and Kate both cater to a different need, what need does she cater to and what can't she offer? What she'd like most is for Gabe to see her writing, but only the stuff she hasn't done yet.

She should text him.

The unspoken rule has been that he gets in touch, maybe just for sex. Texting him first, for no practical reason, feels like the start of something different, a question about what might be available between meetings, and in general. Even the idea of contacting him begins to infuse the weekend with something it's already lacking.

She goes for a casual:

Back at beach—brisk, but carcass-free.

Her fourth draft. Still hateful.

It also occurs to her, after the message has gone, that brisk wasn't a thing between them, just something Gabe had said, and she had dwelt on. The word choice seems bizarre without this context. Geriatric, even.

So, who's feeding the cat? Addie asks.

After a pause.

Just a neighbour, says Dylan.

No one is feeding the cat. This must be obvious. Its food is on a timer, but presumably it needs water? She could have asked Gabe, which would have been a brisk-free reason to text, and he'd have been in and out of her place too, looking around, filling her in, with Anna, of course, but still.

When's Sasha getting here? Clark asks, casually returning the wicker ball to Gabi.

For dinner, Addie says, pretending not to notice.

She's spreading sheets of pink newspaper over the counter. Finally, a use for her *FT*.

Her boyfriend's driving them up, she adds. Hope that's okay,

Dylan? She's only in town for another week and we have the space.

Dylan barely knows Sasha, Addie's youngest sister, which makes her frustrated with Matt for a conversation which may or may not have happened in which he said yes to everything. But it's hard not to admire Addie's effect on him, the two of them now pulling a lobster out of his cardboard box, holding it up, one taped claw each, like some monstrous, deformed baby.

Sure, she says. Is that thing alive?

Yes, says Matt. They can live for twenty-four hours in the cooler.

That's barbaric.

Matt lowers the first lobster onto the newspaper, pulls a second from the box.

They won't be in there long, says Addie. Also, lobsters don't feel pain.

You know this how? asks Dylan.

She's right, Javi says, their brains aren't complex enough to process pain in the same way as ours. If they look like they're reacting to things like intense heat, or cold, it's just a reflex.

Good to know, but has anyone actually asked one?

One what?

A lobster—whether it feels pain? Claustrophobia in a cooler? I mean, it's fair to say no one can know for sure what a lobster does and does not feel.

She sounds absurd. Her absurdity is a physical presence in the room; small but potent, like the wicker ball. Matt's expression confirms this. He has the second lobster casually draped over his right hand, like one of those overconfident dads you see holding their kids in ways which don't seem safe. That guy at Trader Joe's last week, for example. Tiny kid up on his shoulders, small legs not quite meeting around his neck, clasped together with one dad hand, the same that was holding a bag of something lumpen, substantial, potatoes maybe, phone in the other, pressed to his tilted head. The kid was leaning forward, just slightly, which seemed to be what made the whole arrangement possible, but what if it jerked suddenly, or leant back? She'd watched them all the way to the register, imagined the kid lying there, wrong-shaped on the linoleum floor, dad suddenly aware of the weight-lessness around his neck, something non-potato gone from his hand.

Matt now lowers the lobster, claws first, onto the paper Addie has laid out, dampened, ready to swaddle.

Ten

At the table, they are eating figs wrapped in prosciutto.

It was supposed to be monkfish wrapped in prosciutto, but monkfish is out of season, or it's still the off-season for that fishmonger, or something else is unseasonal. Addie is looking at Dylan as she explains this, as though she is the thing that is out of season—born five days late, in fact, but still too early for monkfish. There are little dishes of salmon roe too, spaced at regular intervals along the table. Matt's idea. He frequently watches her scrape it off her sushi to enjoy on its own. This is a thing between them, he must believe; the scraping of roe, the noticing of scraping of roe. Their first date had been at Sushi on Hudson— his choice. He'd made a comment about the restaurant's name being unimaginative, then went on to order cucumber mini rolls followed by avocado mini rolls. She figured he must be one of those people in it for the soy, but he hadn't gone near it, so the joyless fact of his order stood. Now he's watching her spoon roe onto a white crust, thinking how well he knows her, liking thinking this, as the rest of the table starts on their not-monkfish wrapped in prosciutto.

They agree not to talk about work, or the news.

They discuss work, then Europe, then Trump.

The British will leave, says Javi.

Also, Trump will run.

Also, Trump will win.

Meanwhile, we've joined Chelsea Piers, says Clark, so Javi can practise on the climbing walls.

Forks sound loud on plates for a while.

Clark then suggests the fish name game, surprised no one has heard of it. He explains how you replace part of a celebrity's name with seafood—like, say, Minnow Driver . . . Clam Kardashian.

Super addictive, he adds.

There's a split second in which people try to decide whether the game is childish, then pin-drop silence as they attempt to top Clam Kardashian.

Roseanne Char

Marlin Brando

Crab Pitt

Addie tries to shut the game down a few times. There's already a fig where monkfish should be, now Clam Kardashian in place of real conversation.

Cod Stewart

Eva Prawn

Javi scans the table . . . Hitler's wife?

Eventually, Dylan comes up with Dame Judi Tench, which arrives so suddenly and brilliantly that it threatens to change the shape of the whole weekend. The game is agreed to have peaked here until Sasha's boyfriend Dom, who is otherwise yet to contribute, debuts the All-American fish family of Kurt Mussel, Goldie Prawn and Skate Hudson, to an almost standing ovation. Dylan presses her fork into the soft flesh of her remaining fig. It is scandalously in season.

When she looks up from her plate, Dom is looking back at her, as if trying to reinforce the connection they'd made about half an hour ago, in the utility room. Dylan had been sent out for ice and he'd followed. She sat on the counter while he scooped ice into a bucket and described the app he's working on, which measures your carbon footprint as you make it. She asked whether it then suggests ways to offset. Whether it had made suggestions today, to him, for example, in one of three cars driving from Manhattan. He seemed to enjoy the abuse because the next thing he did was to cup her dangling calf, quite suddenly, as though it seemed to him in danger of falling. This was a shock, in the way that sexual attention is always a shock, but also because her legs have never been a feature. They're only on display tonight because Sally forced her into this dress— bohemian, she'd said, before laughing like that was a laughable thing to say, or a laughable look, or because something else was funny.

Still, Dylan had let Dom, for a while, cup her white calf.

It was a gentle kind of cupping, which became light pressing, then a brushing kind of stroking, moving up past the knee before she removed his hand, exaggerating her shock, as though anything below the knee were a normal part of going to get ice.

Dom then exaggerated his apology, almost bowing at one point, and the whole pantomime falseness of the situation had been so relaxing that when he then produced a hash cookie—in sad shrink wrap, like a snack for recess—she'd thought why not. Afghan, he explained, so strong, which hadn't appealed, and dark chocolate, which had. It's had no obvious effect on either of them other than to establish, for Dom, clearly, some kind of tenuous bond above and beyond cupping. This is the thing he's looking for her to validate as she hands her plate to Clark and tries to make a delicious starter face at Addie, who is looking over from the opposite head of the table. She'd seated everyone in that showy way hosts do when they want to give the impression of some grand vision at work. Matt is sitting next to Addie, which is presumably one hundred per cent of her vision. She's tilting her head towards him now, parting her lips just slightly, the way she does when she's sort of listening but mostly trying to work out how to dovetail something from her own experience into the story being told. Matt's making it difficult for her to achieve this as he's up and down a lot getting condiments, paper towels, meeting people's needs.

Are people okay?

Could they be more okay?

Eventually he makes his way over to Dylan.

Is she having a good time?

He lingers behind her as he asks this then squeezes her shoulders in a way that feels surprisingly complicit. Like now things are underway he can admit he always knew this would be the kind of weekend she'd hate, but this is the world they live in, and he doesn't like it any more than she does, and wouldn't everyone here, if they're honest, rather be somewhere else, or with some-one else, or doing something else? Aren't most people just going along with most things most of the time? She leans back into his giant torso, which is just the right amount of hard and soft, think-ing how if he said, I love you, right now, she'd say it back and it wouldn't be a lie. When she turns to face him, he's signalling to Addie, gesturing in the direction of a large silver tureen, not thinking about what the world is like, in fact, nor how everything is compromise—squeezing her shoulders to check whether she's ready to behave like a normal person, or would she still like to ask the lobster how it feels?

Matt joins Dom in the kitchen.

Addie's eyes widen, when the two of them then approach with the tureen, like she's preparing to be surprised by her own lobster-child creation. The rest of the group makes the kind of collective noise they default to whenever Gabi enters the room, which adds to the burgeoning feeling of child sacrifice. Addie as tragic hero, poaching, peeling, plating her offspring, in service of what?

There's bound to be a myth like this.

A retelling of a myth like this.

Matt proceeds to serve the bisque from a fug of sea-steam, chunks of flesh breaking its pink surface. People accept their bowls, pause with their spoons, and the feeling is of a piece of stock imagery.

Friends gathered at beach.

Or else it's adulthood they're performing, which is also the thing they are inside. The house pretending too, with its driftwood sculptures and framed sea views beside real sea views—Dylan there, one half of one too many couples. First Couple, in a sense, this weekend, responsible for delivering something she cannot give. She reaches past her bowl and begins to spoon roe directly into her mouth, separates the eggs with her tongue, the glistening wet of them, finds their bursting point against her teeth.

Roe Farah. Lord Sebastian Roe.

You could do a Gospel service in Harlem, Addie says to Sasha, who's asking for stuff to do in the city—I went to one last Sunday.

Off the red-eye? says Dylan.

Yeah. You know those things last three hours? That's not something they tell you in the programme. Also, they keep you in a pen at the back, if you're not a regular.

Part of the congregation, you mean, says Dylan. And I have sympathy for that.

For what?

I mean, what were you doing there, really?

People go all the time, for the music.

It's not a gig.

I'm aware.

You did just call the order of service a programme.

Order of service, then.

It's a strange sort of voyeurism, really, watching another culture at worship.

Harlem's great, anyway, Matt intervenes, suggesting a few places, most of which have closed.

Dylan fishes a piece of roe out from behind her back tooth, pops it sweetly, wetly.

Then another.

After a while Addie's looking in her direction again, nodding a deep nod.

Aren't you? she says.

She waves her hand then, as if she imagines some kind of conversational motion sensor, flush situation.

What am I?

A big deal in advertising.

This is Sasha's cue to announce she's interested in marketing, an internship, for now, if she can get one.

She's got this mock pitch thing, Addie resumes, as part of the interview at Ogilvy. I thought you could give her some tips?

Addie's looking at Sasha when she says this, clearly deploying Dylan the same way she does at certain parties, when she introduces her as her friend from England, instead of, say, her human woman friend.

I actually quit a while back, says Dylan.

She's grateful no one points out it's only been three weeks.

Four weeks?

Fuck.

But it's not complicated, she obliges. Most clients just want you to tell them they're not in the business they're actually in. Addie could have told you that, it's most of what she does in consultancy. Like, no, Mr Incontinence Pad, you're not in the business of spontaneous urination, but the business of, I don't know, *shame management*. Or take Matt's venture in Femtech . . .

She pauses.

This word never gets the reaction it deserves.

. . . his app presents itself as some kind of fertility hack, offering women more certainty, less uncertainty, whichever tested better, but the business he's in is paranoia. You're counting basically everything, now you get to count your eggs too, viable eggs, whatever, watch their quality dwindle until you are unwoman.

She takes another spoonful of roe.

Sucks it through her teeth.

So that's the reality, she says—she has no idea if this is what the app actually does, or even claims to do—but an agency pitching Matt would tell him he's in the business of, I don't know, The Great American Family, or The Modern, Great American Family, or The New, Modern, Great American Family, if they thought he was interested in awards. That or hitch him to the female empowerment bandwagon, which as we know can accommodate literally anything.

There's silence then, and Matt starts to clear plates.

Uh, yeah. Sasha says. Okay, thanks.

It's not completely clear what point she's ended up making but she had a pleasing feeling of momentum for a while, and there was nodding at some point, from somewhere.

Matt laughs, and the table visibly relaxes.

Thanks for the vote of confidence, he says.

Anyway, says Sally, something like forty per cent of the time the fertility issue lies with the guy.

Exactly, Dylan says—this is new information—who's working on Mantech?

Mentech, Sally improves.

Room full of women, ideally, says Sasha.

This comment should make her more likeable.

YO Sperm, Clark interjects.

Sally laughs one of her massive open laughs and rocks onto the back legs of her chair.

Of course it's Yo Sperm. I suppose you just lie your penis on the screen?

You do not, says Javi.

Anyway, Sally continues, how many guys do you reckon are Yo Sperming who aren't trying to conceive in that moment?

There's a sound like consecutive hiccups then, and Clark moves the iPad that's been at his feet up onto the table, where Gabi now appears on screen, shifting in her bed, like a gratuitous live promotion.

You don't need to put it there, says Javi.

Clark wipes the iPad with his sleeve to better appraise the small mound of his daughter, then leans it against the tureen.

Javi doesn't believe in screens at the table, he says. Screens at all. He thinks the digital revolution is unintellectual.

Javi looks back at him blankly.

When he published his last book, Clark continues, he went onto Amazon to look at reader reviews and it said that people who bought his book also bought Redecker dish washing brush, 4cm, stiff.

Nice, says Javi.

And two replacement heads, says Clark. He asked me whether it meant that more than one person who bought his book had also bought this brush.

Everyone's laughing now, mostly because it is so easy to love Javi in this moment, his bankrolled brain.

I was just interested in the way those recommendations work, he says. Anxious about the book. Bored. I don't know.

You were about to start correlating, Clark says.

Don't be ridiculous.

That's what you do.

Fuck off.

I love your correlations.

Javi says something in Spanish, dodges a kiss from his husband then gets up to check on Gabi, the analogue way.

Anyway, I thought you didn't want kids, says Sally.

This comment is directed at Dylan, and seems to come from nowhere at this point. She and Sally have never discussed the subject conclusively, but the way Sally now lands her chair back in the upright position makes it seem as though they have.

Not having a baby is the bravest thing you can do, she says, instinctively, partly because she's been put on the spot, and partly because she'd like to be the kind of person who felt as strongly as this, about a subject such as this.

It's definitely the greenest thing you can do, says Sasha—Dom, what's the carbon footprint for a baby? I bet your score plummets when you have a kid.

It's not like a credit rating, he says.

Fuck, it should be, says Sally, like if your carbon footprint hits a certain level, you can't get a loan, a mortgage, expand your life in any way.

This starts another circular conversation about data. At one point, Sasha tries to make a connection between *The Handmaid's Tale* and Matt's app, the actual function of which remains unclear, then Dom, who arrived in a 4x4, says it's moot anyway, if we're all going to be underwater in fifty years.

Dylan is only half listening, distracted by delayed feelings of rage at Addie's silence in the previous discussion, pretending to be disengaged, marking her separateness in this way.

The main thing is to take action before you hit thirty-eight, she interrupts. Right, Addie?

Matt pauses with a stack of plates.

Action on what?

Dylan glances at the wall clock, its lighthouse hands.

I guess mine are done in twenty minutes?

Your what?—Matt again.

Eggs. Ovaries, is it?

Addie looks at her with open horror.

Do you think we'll hear them go? Sally intervenes.

What? says Dylan.

Your ovaries. Roevaries. Madame Roevary.

It can't be a fictional person, Clark says.

Brian Nemo, Sally tries.

The fish can't be fictional.

For fuck's sake.

Sally picks up her glass and heads out for a smoke.

Other conversations resume, while Dylan dips her finger-tips into the large pillar candle in front of her. She waits for the sting, the stiffening, then drops another wax fingerprint into the growing pile on her side plate. She's trying to figure out how to do her thumb when, Fuck, then a crash comes from the kitchen, where Addie has apparently found cloudy glasses in the dishwasher. Clark jokes about someone needing the Redecker, 4cm, stiff, so there's laughter over the first part of her outburst, which is directed at the dishwasher, initially, like it's the reason she chose this house, Sag, this group of people, but her disappointment quickly mushrooms into something so epic that it cannot be contained by this small, neat cube of appliance, mouth open in protest, powerless against the brute force of—what even is this?—that is so mesmerising it takes a while for anyone to notice her hand.

Oh, shit, says Sasha.

Addie looks over at her sister, then the blood on the countertop, then her hand.

I broke a glass, she says. I think. Must have, in the sink.

She stares into her open palm, briefly, then stretches it towards the group, cupping her pooling blood in a way that makes it seem like some kind of offering. There's silence, for a moment, and the feeling they should look away, then Matt is up and around the counter, balling Bounty into her hand, like he's trying to hide the wound rather than seal it. Moments later, Dom comes to life, unwrapping Matt's dressing, running Addie's hand under the tap to get a better look, and, yeah, he says, you're going to need stitches, but it looks like a clean cut.

Two years of pre-med, Sasha manages to divulge, before joining her sister in the kitchen. Dom rewraps Addie's hand in a clean dishcloth, Sasha pours her a glass of water and Matt offers to run her over to A&E. Addie is eerily silent as these things happen, arms outstretched, Christlike. Something compelling in her pose. Something else coming off her too, which is hard to pin down

108

due to the loud braying noise that has started up elsewhere in the room, like a cartoon donkey.

Some game of Gabi's?

She scans the living room, then table, where no one is looking for this noise, only at her, the origin of this noise, this laughter, now increasing in volume, possessing her completely, so that it's hard to catch her breath, or hear exactly what anyone is saying when Javi arrives back in the room, asking what's happened.

A hijacking, is the answer. She, readying to detonate, Addie somehow already caught in the blast, achieving the thing she cannot—actually bleeding out.

Actually.

Impossible to convey this through her laughter, which is working independently now, like a spasm or a contraction, performing some necessary function outside of her control. She glances over at Matt, who is red-faced and shaking, about to speak, it looks like, when Addie launches herself past him, air-bound seeming as she heads across the living space towards her.

Mind the cushions, she says.

Addie stops.

The beginning of a smile on her lips becomes a grimace as she unwinds her dressing and wipes her hand along the full length of the sofa. She holds eye contact with Dylan as she does this, then leaves through the front door. Dom then Sasha follow. Matt grabs his keys and gives her a look she hasn't seen before. She thought she'd seen all of the looks, which makes this one kind of a turn-on.

As the front door closes, the deck door opens.

Sally back from her smoke.

Where is everyone? What's funny?

There's a brief silence, before something then shoots out of the lighthouse clock, some kind of deranged, seafaring cuckoo ushering in her birthday. She gathers her wax fingerprints, walks them past Sally and into the bathroom, where she presses a fist into the soft area below her chest, and takes a breath. Directly in front of her, on the shelf above the sink, there's a to-go coffee cup. Printed on this, some kind of reverse mermaid or fish woman on her knees, which she has, instead of a tail, and a fish head, and shells over her large, scaly breasts. She is wearing a rubber ring, or trapped inside it, arms pinned to her sides, swollen fish lips puckered. Dylan stares into her bug-eyes for a while, then drops her fingerprints into the cup.

The laughter fully gone from her body.

Later, she and Matt have sex.

Fight, then have sex. This is unexpected, and fraught, to begin with, then tender and confusing. Matt has to pull out, as she forgot her pill, but they both still come, almost together, which rarely happens. Afterwards, they lie in silence, Matt on his side of the bed, she on hers.

A door opens in the corridor.

Tuna Turner, someone shouts out.

The door bangs shut.

Eleven

New York is everyone touching themselves, all of the time.

Last week, that guy on Bleecker, three A.M., between the Marc Jacobses. Now, some guy at the back of the IFC, watching *Not I*—giant, disembodied mouth projected onto the screen in front of him. Waiting for a cock, does he think it is?

His dick is literally still out, Sally tells the usher, as they leave.

A relief, she's here. A week now, since everyone leaving Sag early, spent mostly ghosted. Clark the first to break ranks, on Thursday:

Unnecessary, he texted.

Then:

Borderline psychotic

Addie's still not picking up, and Matt hasn't called since he got back to San Francisco. Sally stayed out of it, mostly, then showed up tonight, unannounced. Here to give her shit, she said, then take her out. They skipped the first thing for Mars Bar, then deep culture, they decided, after a few hours of drinking.

Beckett, therefore, at the IFC.

MDMA outside Beckett at the IFC.

Other things that are unclear. Grilled cheese at The Odeon—twice—and dancing at Gold Bar. Or sleeping on the banquettes there? She'd grabbed for the cab door, definitely, at one point, certain she was having an anxiety attack. More Molly, Sally's prescription for this.

The next morning, they do short stack pancakes before Sally's train at Penn. Nothing lonelier than Penn Station, she's always thought, or is thinking now, for the first time, too shredded to tell.

Walking home, a text from Matt:

I don't know what to say

Also:

You're a strange mood

He does not correct the typo.

She screenshots both and sends them to Sally.

Passive proactive, Sally replies, the next morning.

What?

If you were a mood

Twelve

Super flower blood moon? Gabe says, and holds out his hand.

This has come right after a super blood wolf moon.

And a super worm equinox moon.

The moon people are beginning to seem desperate, like moon stock is down.

Gabe suggests they check it out from the roof; our roof, he says, which of course they share, can't avoid sharing, but still feels good when he says it. He'd shown up while she was making noodles, a dark halo behind her own blown-out reflection in the fire-escape glass—taller, broader, clearly other—and it's a rush she'd felt, more than anything, even before she understood it was him, in black boots and jacket, crying moon.

We'll take the gooseneck, he says, gesturing at the ladder running up past the roofline, curling over. Gooseneck, he explains, is the name for a ladder running up past the roofline, curling over, but she's happy to chalk the term up to him. She wants him a lot when he says things like this, already knows exactly the kind of word or phrase which, from him, will activate this feeling.

Too much hooch

Dog days of summer

After Coney she told him she'd seen a roach in her kitchen, huge, like some kind of baby dinosaur, and he said he'd set up a roach motel. A motel for roaches. It's a brand, as it turns out, ROACH MOTEL in yellow 3D caps all over the black boxes he brought over—*Roaches check in, but they don't check out*—though it barely matters as she's already logged it a certain way. Her complicity in this kind of thing makes her feel pretty easy, which she finds she doesn't mind, quite likes, if she's honest. Now she leans back and looks up for evidence of something worm-moony, like if she goes with him, that's why she'll be going. Like she wouldn't go if he'd just said hey, or nothing at all.

It's mostly cloud, but she takes his hand anyway.

Up the gooseneck with Gabe.

He goes first, then pulls her up the last bit, which she doesn't need and makes her feel like she's going to fall. He leaves white pressure marks on her wrists, and she wonders how it might feel to be held tighter, for longer. The other night she'd woken with his arm pressing into her cheekbone and she'd pressed back, imagining a bruise, the possibility of a bruise, wondering what's the tipping point.

Up top everything is white. Brickwork, satellite dishes, exhaust ducts, all white. Even the surfacing is painted a sort of off-white, which gives the whole thing the feeling of a child's school project; some kind of mission control or space station built from whatever's to hand then sprayed over. Gabe finds a spot by a low wall, towards the middle of the roof, and takes beers and a blanket out of his duffel. He empties his pockets onto the blanket—tobacco, cigarette papers, lighter—then sits and hands Dylan a bottle. The cardboard carrier is from that store on Broadway, with the Mix & Match. She gets six of the same when she goes, but Gabe's got all different, it looks like, which must make him the most something and her the least. Or her the most and him the least. It's the same place that has the Tostitos she likes, with a hint of lime, but only the massive bag, the one that's the size of a pillowcase, which was shocking to her, when she first arrived in the city, but she's picked one up a few times now, mostly for the skanky, shameless feeling of carrying it home on a Saturday night, across Fifth, up Greenwich, past the tables outside Rosemary's, couples lifting pink slivers of meat from white china, pressing it to her chest like some wrong lover or obese pet.

They sip for a while in silence.

He sits, she stands.

They agree the moon is nothing much; there, clearly, behind a bit of cloud, full, and maybe closer than usual. Silence again, then a single bass note drifting over from a roof party on the other side of East Third; low-lit, DJ, obnoxious-seeming, yet certain of itself in a way her evening with Gabe does not seem to be, already, set beneath a moon that is nothing much, but also, maybe, closer. She senses she will have to fill in for this moon-lack, feels this quite strongly as she walks towards the sound, which is more of a vibration, making it almost to the edge of the building before she remembers the shapeless cardigan she's wearing, was wearing when Gabe caught her off-guard in the kitchen, now thinking how it must look from behind, how removing it would be impossible to do naturally at this point, everything determined by her next move, which cannot be to draw attention to this sad garment, stretched out over her ass, pockets sagging like imposter body parts, confirming, should there be any doubt, that she is not fit to understudy the moon, barely fit to understudy herself.

Wish you were at the other gig? Gabe asks.

She lets the question inflate like a life raft.

Naturally, she then says, and turns to find him hunched over a piece of cigarette paper, sprinkling tobacco, raising and lowering his hand like he's seasoning a tiny burrito—not looking in her direction, showing no moon-lack at all. He wets the paper edge of his creation, and she thinks of licking the lime off a Tostito; the way all the moisture in her body shows up either side of her tongue. She would, in this moment, do anything he asked.

On her way back to the blanket, she stops to take in the tangle of old TV antennas by the exhaust duct—

a broadcast

a communication

a confusion?

Does it speak to anything now, she says, this kind of antenna?

Gabe looks over.

I don't think so, he says. Not anymore.

A silence then, of antennas.

His cigarette makes a crisp, fizzing sound as he lights up and she sits and tells him about a project a friend of hers consulted on back in the UK, years ago, some piece of media research where they asked a bunch of housewives to give up their radios and keep a video diary about the experience. He looks away, towards the East River, as though he finds her friend's media background as gross as she finds her friend's media background, which is also her media background, her grossness.

Huh, he then says. Or, and?

Total devolution, she says, within days in some cases. Only four women made it past the first week. Isn't that crazy?

I don't know.

He picks a piece of tobacco off his lip.

We all have our filler stuff.

She'd meant the two of them to observe this behaviour sad-poetically, from a distance, but can sense herself becoming implicated.

Gabe leans back on his elbows.

Sometimes I'm sickened by my own hypocrisy.

She resists the urge to find this riveting.

Waits for him to elaborate.

Nothing.

The observation is an end in itself; some little character dropping he's choosing to leave now and can return to whenever, like I did tell you this about myself, pointing at the hard, pellety fact of it. And yet it is riveting, sickened by my own hypocrisy, because what does he mean?

Yours is books, he then says, or asks.

My what?

Your filler. The book situation in your apartment is insane.

She's happy with this observation, despite the fact it has the word insane in it and it's Anna's book situation he's observing. She counters with a comment about his lack of books, unaware she'd taken inventory too.

There's literally nothing with pages in your apartment.

Gabe frowns.

That whole back wall in the bedroom is a bookcase—those cupboards open upwards.

She pictures the sheer, white expanse he's referring to. Its faint criss-crossing lines she'd read as some kind of design detail.

That's perverse, she says.

What is?

Hiding your books.

I'm not hiding my books.

It feels like you are.

He's laughing now. She might be too, if these words weren't coming from her, caught out suddenly, by what? Not his books, but his hidden booksness is the thing that seems to threaten their dynamic somehow, whatever space she'd planned to carve out within it. That they had some special kind of moon in Sag, is what she says next, which makes no sense when they could be talking about the books they've read, or are reading, or plan to read, which would give her a better chance of showing him the thing (what thing?) she needs him to see, or know about, if he hasn't twigged yet.

I don't think so, he says.

She sips her beer; bitter, more hoppy than she's used to.

Pretty sure we did.

They hadn't made it to the moon in the end, to looking out for it, though Addie had mentioned it, again, in the car on the way over.

Gabe shakes his head.

Some kind of moon expert, Gabe must be.

March moon was rare, he offers. Once in a lifetime, they said.

Did they? she says, and wonders who is Gabe's they.

Whether it's a BuzzFeed they, say, or a *Times* they. Some other kind of they. He frowns when she says something about the end of the world, so:

Hottest July, she clarifies, polar vortex, once-in-a-generation moon . . .

Gabe moves his cigarette into his left hand, then reaches over with his right and tucks her hair behind her ear, like you would to someone who was cute but didn't know things, or cute but hadn't seen things. He goes on to explain basic moon cycles and their non-relationship to global warming. She'd been going for symbolism, clearly, but finds she's happy to submit to the moon-splain, as he's now using terms like moonrise and moonset, which are of course a thing, but she's never encountered before, so it feels like he's introducing her to new parts of the day, thirty-eight years into her experience of days.

Everything's fucked, though, he agrees. Clearly.

The East River had frozen in February, not solid, but there were chunks of ice floating down its length, like a scene from some disaster movie. There had been a duck with its feet frozen into Bethesda Fountain too, a colleague announced, while the whole office trawled for posts about the most freakish bits of frozen city. It didn't seem possible, the duck thing, but that was the image which stuck, more than actual Armageddon outside the window, feeding dreams where she'd wake up unable to move her legs for seconds that felt like minutes. Sleep paralysis, her doctor said, disinclined to put a duck lens on things—not uncommon. It's *Orlando* that springs to mind now; Woolf's young woman struck by a blast of ice, turned to powder, blown over the rooftops in a puff of dust. Opposite energy to the duck situation, which Gabe says is highly unlikely, when she describes it.

They're quiet for a while then, considering the fuckedness of things together, or other things separately. On the other side of Third, the bass note has jumped an octave, a few octaves, taut now, as though she could walk along it and drop into the other evening quite easily. Gabe ashes into his bottle top then lies on his side. His black duffel gapes open behind him, revealing a crumpled tub, two crumpled tubs, something Betty Crocker? Big red spoons on the side.

Are your parents still together? he says.

They are.

He nods.

You seem like someone whose parents would be together.

She knows this about herself, fears it, without being able to say what it is she fears.

Why do you think that is? he goes on.

Why do I think my parents are together or why do I seem the way I seem?

The first thing, he says, like it's obvious why she seems the way she seems.

That's a weird question.

You don't find it interesting, why people stay together?

This is an invitation, surely, to ask about his and Kate's togetherness, but she does not do this, instead says, quite instinctively, that her parents decided to be together. The answer arrives swiftly, emphatically, as if stored away long ago, waiting for the question. It sounds stark, brutal even, said out loud like this—they decided—full of maybe-pain and compromise. Gabe's parents had separated eventually, he explains, long after he left home. Mostly because of the situation with his uncle. He was closer to Walter by then anyway, a friend of his grandfather's, let him crash at his place in Red Hook from time to time. Bellhop in the city, he'd been, back in the day.

Which hotel? she asks, pointlessly.

Freelance, he says. Used to show up along Central Park East, open cab doors, pocket the tip. A girlfriend of his made uniforms for a few of them and took a cut of the profits. Not a bad gig, apparently, while it lasted.

Gabe flicks away the butt of his cigarette and sits up, which feels like her cue to share some family quirk, or side hustle, or story of childhood, but only the moons back home come to mind, just the normal ones, unadvertised, how bright they'd get in the dark countryside; moonlight bouncing off the spoons on the breakfast table when she'd go down for water sometimes, an actual glare. Too provincial to share after phony bellhops on Central Park East. Something to do with the cutlery element. Or the table already laid for breakfast is the thing which feels small.

Gabe scoops her in then and starts to run his hand down the back of her neck, over the bumps on her spine, one, two, like he had at Coney, rerouting her thoughts from moonglare to that asterisk cloud, his dick through wet underpants, the weight of the sand on her chest, thrilling now, after the event.

What did you mean by, 'stuff like that', she says, when you talked about making ends meet in the city?

His hand keeps moving . . . three . . . four . . .

Life modelling and 'stuff like that', is what you said.

Gabe's face does something strange, which she scans, then stores, so she can just submit to the fact of it now. She lowers her head to make room for his hand to continue, but he takes it back and starts to build a new smoke. He's quiet for a moment, doing this, then offers up a story about his first time life modelling. He'd heard from a friend, he says, that posing for artists was a thing you could do to make rent, totally kosher, the one he was sitting for that day—Figure Drawing 101, it was called, in this old studio in Queens. Only five people showed up for it, all older guys, him on a wooden stool, butt naked up on this small platform. Halfway through the time he was supposed to change positions but must have shifted in a strange way, because the stool came off the platform, with him on it, and brought him down hard. There was a drawn-out silence when he first came off, or that's how it felt, body splayed like that, dick flopped out in front of him— she pictures his dick, tries to imagine it younger—which is when you think someone would get up, but nobody did. He was pretty badly banged up, deep gash on his leg, but he needed the money, so got himself back into position and the class carried on sketching. The wound was bleeding steadily, sending blood down his shin, between his toes, but no one offered him something to patch himself up, or even moved a muscle.

The story feels like it should go somewhere next, but he stops, rolls up the right leg of his pants and runs her hand along the groove in his shin, which is deep, deliberate seeming, like a notch carved into wood. He looks up then, as though he'd like her to tell him what the episode might have meant, or just to check whether that's the kind of story she was after, like it's one of many stories he could have told, like he's sickened by his own hypocrisy, like he knows a good beach to bury a girl. She presses her finger gently into the space he's showing her, where there are special nerve endings and he feels everything. Or nothing? Either way, it occurs to her that it's the kind of space she might fit herself into. Where her vagueness might be recast in his particulars.

Suddenly, the sound of chairs being dragged along the other roof. This makes her self-conscious, and she picks up Gabe's cigarette papers for something new to do with her hand. When he reaches over, she's ready to have it returned to his leg, but instead he pulls out a sheet of rice paper, lights it and tosses it upwards. She watches it bloom then disappear, bloom as it disappears, eat itself, gone. She pulls out a second, which he lights as she lets it go. Another violent bloom. They carry on like this for a while, her producing papers—satisfying click as each new edge appears—Gabe setting them alight, coming close to her fingers only once, when she fails to let go, finding their rhythm quickly after that, sending up Rizla fireflies, gorging on their split-second life cycle. She'd thought he might do something impulsive like fuck her up here. A promised violence, in his sudden appearance, in black boots and jacket, but they're getting somewhere different now, she can tell, as she produces another paper, then another, until Gabe's like, hey leave me something to smoke, and they stop.

Bodies continue to arrange themselves along the opposite roof, as Hepburn's giant, light-filled head takes shape on the grey brick of the facing wall.

Suckers, says Gabe, and she really wants him.

Hopper's brought snacks, he adds, and seconds later Hopper appears from Gabe's side of the blanket dragging the corpse of something unreadable, a thin wet trail appearing behind it. A few feet in front of them, Hopper drops the creature—a small bird—and starts to wrestle its head from the huddled roundness of its body. She coughs up a mouthful of beer then looks for something to wipe her chin.

You don't have a tissue, do you?

Gabe hunches forward, as though preparing to stroke the cat, or what's left of the bird.

Why do you say it like that?

Like what?

. . . you don't, do you . . .

British tick, I guess.

To assume the worst? Or is the idea to keep the stakes low?

There's a grim wrenching sound, as Hopper stretches his back legs and walks off with the bird's head.

Would it be so bad, Gabe says, if you asked, do you have a tissue and I said no? Like, what do you think would happen?

Okay, do you have a tissue?

No, he says. Who has a tissue?

He grins and leans over to lick the beer from her chin. This is fundamentally disgusting, the cloying wetness he leaves behind, the way it's meant to clean her up, but something in the way he draws back makes her lean forward and offer herself again. He draws his tongue up, slowly this time, stiffening slightly as it meets hers. Over his left shoulder, Hopper is playing with the bird's head, batting it between wet paws.

Cute cat, she thinks, starting to get the way things work, could work, with Gabe, other things too. How anything can be whatever.

/

A book a day, is the plan.

Working through the shelf above Anna's bed in the early morning, now she's waking with the light, the street cleaner, noise from Avenue A.

In the Lispector:

I have unglued myself from me

also:

I, like the instant, spark and go out

She underlines these rightnesses as they come, keep coming, along with the feeling a rightness always brings, that nervous energy, hard to metabolise.

Coffee, then.

And another.

Out on the fire escape, dawn sky purpling like a black eye.

Death is like the waiting colon, Lispector says.

And life, she adds, in pencil, as this is not her copy.

Back in bed—
In the early hours I awake full of fruit, she underlines
and
Who will come to gather the fruit of my life?
:
:

Thirteen

Betty Crocker is giving Gabe a hand job.
This is happening on the sidewalk opposite Three Lives bookstore.
It is furious and beginnery and seems as though it may never end.
Dylan is inside Three Lives, watching through the glass store-
front. Gabe is indifferent. He is holding Betty's red spoon, like
a paddle at an auction. Betty is determined. She changes hands
a lot and does not stop when a ringing begins, amplified through
speakers where streetlamps should be. Gabe looks up, sees Dylan,
waving now, through the glass storefront, hoping not to be seen,
calling out—hey Gabe, hey Betty—hoping not to be heard.
A bookseller appears, with instructions, he says.
For the hand job? The ringing?
He hands her a book.
She takes a moment to feel the weight of it.
Opens it—wider.
Listens to the spine crack.

★

When she wakes, Sally is on the phone.

I've tried you three times.

I was sleeping, she says, dream pressed up against her still.

It's three in the afternoon.

She glances at the window, sun pushing in through muslin drapes.

I took one of the blue ones.

Blue ones what?

From that bottle.

Sally found the pills when they got back from Sag, was barely through the door before she was opening drawers, cupboards, looking for something good—her words.

When did you take it?

Noon-ish.

How are you even functioning?

I only took half.

Sally says nothing then, like half stacks up, half is her thing.

She kicks her sheet off, props her head on a pillow.

Is Betty Crocker real?

Sorry?

A baking, human woman or just a face on a packet?

Face thing, surely.

What's the tub with the red spoon?

Isn't that all of them?

I think it's cookie dough, she's suggesting, when a kind of panting or groaning starts up at the other end of the line, a little distance from the phone.

She waits.

Wonders if she should hang up.

Sorry, Sally says, eventually. Dan's dog lives in my crotch.

Cute.

Really likes to get his nose up in there when I'm bleeding.

This would be disturbing even if she didn't know how intense Sally's periods can be. How interactive too. They briefly shared an apartment where the bathroom came right off the sitting room, its door invariably left open for Sally's shitting, shaving, showering. She'd pulled out a tampon once, while they were talking, left it swinging in her hand as she finished whatever she was saying, laughing when she noticed the size of the blood clot clinging to it, lifting it higher to admire its crimson grimness. She had to supplement with sanitary towels usually, day and night, extra-long, which she'd half-heartedly roll then leave unfurling in the trash, like some grotesque stop-motion flower.

Dan thinks it's hilarious, of course, Sally goes on. Like he'd be perfectly happy if the dog spent two weeks of every month trying to penetrate him.

There's the sound of wind on the receiver now.

Where are you?

We only get decent reception at the end of the track. Some farmer dug into the cable. It's pretty much the one cable for the whole area.

This doesn't tally with the barn conversion Dylan imagined, has had to imagine, as Sally's not one for detail. She adjusts this visual, pictures Sally barefoot now, for some reason, toes curled into wet earth, like some Manson girl. The one who's basically running the gig.

She's worth two million dollars, by the way, she says.

Who?

Betty Crocker.

She's real?

Face on a packet.

Right.

Is two million dollars high or low, do you think, in the baking world? Post-tax.

You mean for a fictional person?

Sally says this like, are you mentally well, then asks if she's spoken to Addie yet.

We're good, she says.

Okay . . .

I apologised.

And?

She suggested I see a life coach.

Sally laughs.

She also asked if I was depressed.

Are you depressed?

No.

How do you know?

Are you depressed?

No.

Okay then.

She worships you, Sally says, is the issue. Also, her mother's a cunt. Hasn't called Addie in a month then sends me an email this morning—*Aadya is struggling*.

How does she know?

Sasha, presumably, reporting from Sag. Anyway, her mother's always been a cunt to her. We have this in common. Had this in common. Cunty mothers. Different, but equally cunty.

This critique makes her flinch. Not because Sally's mother died, but because of the way she feels about her own mother.

On Addie's side, Sally continues, she's got the immigrant parent thing, but with a twist—brutally demanding, yet somehow totally disinterested on an emotional level. My mother just ignored me until I was old enough for boyfriends, then tried to fuck them. It's not even original, which she was, actually, I'll give her that.

This kind of concession is rare. Though Sally did seem almost proud once, after a night of drinking, describing her mother's stint at the Chelsea Hotel. She'd lived there with a famous puppet maker, who'd taught her the craft and helped her start her own business. Then she meets Sally's father, who moves them to Chicago and leaves right after her brother turns two. From then on, everything's about the business, making freakishly lifelike dolls for grown women who can't have kids. Some creepy underground market Sally doesn't get into explaining, propped up by her mother, who completely neglected her own kids in the process. She died ten years ago, of ovarian cancer. Sally only found out because her stepfather invited her to the memorial. She didn't go.

I'm selling shitbox, by the way, Sally says. Did I tell you?

Seriously?

Renters are going end of the month, then I'm selling.

Shitbox is the apartment her mother left her. The crumbling studio on Sullivan she was living in when Dylan first met her.

I kind of love that place, says Dylan.

It's a good time to sell, says Sally. Close that chapter.

The New York chapter, does she mean? The mother chapter?

Anyway, Sasha's the only sibling that shows an interest, Sally says, back on Addie. A little shit, as you know, very manipulative. And Addie goes along with it because . . . I don't know why. Probably she's figured out most New York friendship ends in disappearance, which is why she makes such a business of it: work, work casual, weekday social, weekend. She's hedging. Like, who's most likely to stick?

What are we?

HQ, I guess. If we tap out, the whole system collapses.

Hard to say whether Sally cares at all what kind of friendship might stick. Sally, who loves the churn and likely chose Dylan precisely for her non-stick qualities. In some ways their friendship is unlikely. Like most friendships are in some way unlikely. As much an act of choosing as love. Often just as brutal.

Sally grinds her lighter, continues:

Addie needs you to corroborate her version of you.

Of her, don't you mean?

The two are related.

How?

She needs to be able to buy what you're selling.

Selling?

About yourself, the city . . . nothing what it seems . . . life as some gorgeously complex nut to be cracked.

Even as she considers protesting, she's aware of some truth in this, a filter she has with Addie, that's quite subtle. Some way of serving up her day-to-day experience that scratches an itch for both of them.

And you have no effect on her at all?

It's her dream and her nightmare, I think, she and I landing a few blocks apart.

How so?

Impossible to try herself on—I've known her too long.

Sally works in the opposite way for Dylan. Makes unfixedness seem like a viable option.

Anyway, you encourage her, Sally goes on. These are the repercussions. You can't decide you find it oppressive now you're changing the brief.

To what?

You tell me.

Sally pauses—

I think you're grateful too, she says.

Okay.

That you get to be relieved you're not her.

Jesus, Sally.

I think you find it helpful, not consciously. I know you love her, both things can be true.

I wouldn't mind a little narrative control over my own situation, that's all.

Take it, Sally says, before cursing and cutting off the call.

This dog is an actual sexual predator, she says when they reconnect, then explains she actually called to talk about Dan.

The change of topic is a relief, though Sally's never called to talk about a man before. I need to talk about Dan, is what she actually says, which is even more disorienting.

Yeah, so his kid showed up at the door yesterday.

The first image which comes to mind is of a baby in a basket, or a box, or whatever left babies come in.

How are you only telling me this now?

Avery, her name is. She took two trains and a bus to get here. She's only ten.

You never mentioned Dan had kids.

Neither did he.

Seriously?

He's not even here. He's delivering a commission to a couple in Detroit, is still somewhere between there and here. Took the truck so has to drive it back.

So, it's just the two of you?

It was, briefly. She's with her uncle in New Jersey. Dan called his ex and they agreed she and her brother—Jonah, seven, also Dan's kid—would stay with him until Dan's back. I dropped her off yesterday afternoon.

Is it insane to ask where her mother is?

I don't know the whole story, just that she has rough patches, is going through one now, rougher than usual.

Okay.

She had this little speech prepared, Dan's kid, about how she and her brother need to live with their dad—just for a while. It was kind of heartbreaking.

That's a lot.

Right.

How did you leave it with Dan?

He wants to talk face to face.

And you?

I'm genuinely interested to hear what he has to say.

Sally says this calmly, rationally, like she really is, genuinely interested, not passive-aggressively interested.

Have you ever seen duck faeces? she then says.

I have not.

They're basically human-sized. We're not even near water, I have no idea where they're coming from.

What if it's not the ducks?

You mean what if my boyfriend takes shits on the track?

Hearing Sally refer to Dan as her boyfriend is somehow more shocking than the idea he might be taking regular dumps in public.

Anyway, I think I want to hear him out, she adds.

Then hear him out.

This is the kind of straightforward advice Sally would offer and is surprisingly easy to emulate. The hiss of her cigarette makes the air seem cold where she is, and crisp. This is the moment to tell her about Gabe, surely. One person shares, the other shares back.

He's married then? she'd probably say.

Then something like:

Not that I care, but you do.

Do I?

You seem like you would.

Conventional, Sally would mean, is how she seems. Like someone whose parents would still be together.

You're loyal, she'd clarify, or think, ideally.

Matt wouldn't come up, which makes her feel bad for him, even though he hasn't actually been discounted, as the Sally conversation isn't actually happening, and would almost certainly not happen in this way. Anyway, the issue is not what Sally might say, or think, or what Dylan should have shared by now, but that Gabe seems to resist integration of any kind. She's tried to imagine him around a table with family and friends a few times, but can only manage his outline, like summoning a reluctant spirit. It's small too, of course, the thing happening between them, in the scheme of things, but she wouldn't be able to hide its unsmallness to her.

Do you want to know Elle Fanning's net worth? she says instead.

No. Which one is Elle?

I don't know, one of them—a Fanning.

She's followed the link under Betty Crocker to a bot page.

It's quite special. I'm sending now.

Lifestyle of Fanning, Elle

Elle is too much concern to live a great life along with her family in a luxurious home that fortunately made her fetch a better career and her way to lead her life in stunning house. This is the best home that was purchased for herself as well as for her parents who were considered as a *great support for her throughout the flourishing career. This grand house was owned by her at a worthier price of $2 million with the support of her sister. This house has been boasted with the lavishing room that was adorned with the best architecture as well as the awesome collection of décor that grants stunning appeal to the house in the majestic bedroom as well as dynamic bathroom that was boasted to offer lavishing touch to the house. The kitchen is the grand place that attracts the taste bud of the people so it comprised of the best mode of technological appliance. This enhances the beauty of the house with the closet is connected to the living room and open to the swimming pool area to offer a pleasant experience of enjoyment anytime planned for a party time . . . she also possesses a hay bales measuring approximately 152,941 square ft.*

What do you think she keeps in the lavishing room? Sally says.

Cunts, presumably.

Or a hay bales.

Or a hay bales.

After Sally hangs up, she toasts a bagel;

thinks of writing,

masturbating,

napping again,

listens for sounds of Gabe below, though she knows he's at a gig in Ohio—*I live in Ohio, but I Love New York*. She pictures a map of America and tries to pinpoint Ohio in relation to where she's now standing, just left of the study window. City all garish blues this afternoon, like badly blended eyeshadow. There are fruit flies too, not around the bagel, but her open document—half thing, half a thing—sensing something left out too long.

Tell me, it says in the toolbar, next to the image of a light bulb.

Tell me what you want to do, the words expand.

She clicks on the light bulb.

Double clicks.

Nothing.

Just blank space, the blinking curser.

Fourteen

From the outside, the bar looks like a whorehouse might look in Disneyland. Inside, a narrow stairwell descends into a womb-like space—low ceilings, old beams strung with rainbow-coloured fairy lights and a wet-coat smell Gabe says is there whatever the season. The lights run the full length of the room, dropping down to decorate an old box TV, plugged into nothing, and a red upright piano, five bar stools bolted to the floor around it.

A built-in drinks ledge connects to the wall on either side of the piano and leaning against it is a guy somewhere in his seventies, looks like, telling a story about the Meatpacking back in the day, how they used to get kicked out of Florent on Monday mornings, then pile into the back of the old meat trucks along Gansevoort.

We'd be in there blowing each other, he says, barely room to swing your dick after closing at Crisco's, then after a while the cops would come in to bust things up . . .

It looks like he's going for his drink at this point, but instead he stretches both arms out in front of him like a beggar in a cartoon.

. . . and I'm telling you now—no joke . . . we'd blow the cops.
I mean, come on!

Come *on!*

Ezra, Gabe says, as they pass the piano. Lives here, pretty
much. Kettle of Fish till opening, then here.

He pulls a ten out of a tight roll of bills and slides it onto
the scuffed mahogany that runs the full length of the back wall.
Rising up behind it, a large mirrored mural depicts French and
American revolutionary scenes overlaid with the words *Liberté,
Fraternité, Egalité.* Someone has crossed out the world *Egalité* in
chalk marker.

Part of a government project, Gabe explains, to get artists
back on their feet during the depression.

Why the two revolutions?

Thomas Paine died here—on this plot, I mean.

She's never heard of Thomas Paine.

This must be obvious too because:

These are the times that try men's souls? Gabe says next.

Then:

The American Crisis?

Rights of Man?

This is a game her father likes to play, as though it's the right
clue she must be missing, rather than the fact at hand. Otherwise,
there's sport to be had in establishing the parameters of her not
knowing, which is only not knowing, and should not be confused
with ignorance, the way knowing is confused with intelligence,
all the time. What she needs is to get onto home ground with

Gabe, though it's less and less clear what home ground looks like, in knowing, in whatever.

Propagandist in both revolutions, Gabe concedes, eventually, and scoops a bottle top off the bar, flips it like a coin, as though it's nothing to him who Thomas Paine is, where he died, what Dylan does and doesn't know.

Tyranny and hell, he adds.

Sorry?

What Paine had to say about your lot.

My lot?

The British.

Also an accurate description of this conversation, conversations like this, but that seems fair, she says. When she orders a vodka tonic, the bartender makes a face like he's suppressing a face. Her order? The way she ordered? Sometimes the accent rubs people the wrong way, like it's pretentious to do British, even if you are British—hellish, tyrannical. The bartender keeps the tonic going to the top of the hi-ball, adds a fat wedge of lemon and leaves the spillage. Gabe's taken a call, so she spins her stool to face the handful of regulars, he says it usually is, at this time, before ten on a Tuesday. Ezra's still going, closer to them now, talking to a different crew, or the same crew in different poses, explaining how the place used to be way gayer, how the glory hole's the only thing they ever fix in here, how the west wall used to be called the meat rack—he walks towards it as he says this, arms wide open, like a real estate broker revealing period features.

Come on, he says.

Come *on!*

Can you know your own refrain? Her question, or Gabe's, first time they fucked? That thing he did with her eyebrow afterwards, his stillness in the window. She'd ask him, but doesn't want it to seem like she's storing every conversation, freighting it with meaning. Especially after their failed text exchange in Sag.

Carcass-free? he'd replied, eventually, to her message.

Then:

I don't get it.

As though he'd forgotten the whole thing at Coney. Crabs undressing, their days-long embrace, the way he sought out her snack of flesh in the car, moving his hand just to change gears. It strikes her as shocking, radical even, sitting next to him now, that he should be the thing he is to her, but also in the world like this. A guy who keeps a roll of tens, knows an Ezra, takes a call sometimes.

She starts on her drink, which is warm, as well as strong, as well as flat, while the regulars heckle the elderly pianist, back from a long cigarette break. Some hum, some sing when he starts up with a number from *Follies*, but mostly it's a charged kind of hush that settles over the space—less to do with the music than the performance of the bar, it feels like, of being the kind of person who shows up in the wet smell, to hum, or sing, or be silent, on a Tuesday before ten. Gabe closes his phone, places the silver nugget of it next to his beer.

So, what do you think?

Of what?

You're into Sondheim, right?

How is this the thing he remembers.

Show tunes only, he explains, is the deal here, which doesn't seem like it would be his style, or a place that makes money.

Sondheim, Porter, Rodgers & Hammerstein . . . only the greats.

He laughs when she asks if he plays here, then explains how requests works, the tip jar, how each pianist has their own repertoire, followers who take care of them, and her growing feeling is that she's being had in some way. As though the faux-wooden panelling, were she to push it, would surely fall away, along with the kitsch lanterns sprouting in pairs, people in twos and threes talking beneath them, *rhubarb, rhubarb* ; as though Gabe might turn around at any moment, give everyone a twenty and the whole place would empty itself out, fold itself up, disappear.

The music stops before the singing.

A skitter of rain on the windows at street level.

Gabe presses a finger into the corn nut salt.

So, what's your boyfriend into? he says.

He glances over.

She remains perfectly still.

Matt, you mean?

Right, says Gabe.

She reaches for her phone, as if to locate Matt there, confirm his separateness.

After a pause.

Does he like Sondheim?

It's unclear what's happening suddenly, in this conversation, also in general.

Sure, she says. I mean, no, it's . . . are you actually asking?

Gabe makes a face like obviously not.

Were you going to mention him at some point?

She wakes her phone again, accidentally takes a loud screen shot, puts it down.

I honestly didn't think you'd be interested.

Wow, okay. So, that's . . . really?

He tilts his bottle.

I don't know what to say to that.

He's hurt.

This is validating before it's shocking, like discussing Matt is shocking, what Matt is into, when they have never discussed Kate, who Dylan has met, who lives downstairs, who introduced her to Gabe, is married to Gabe, and must have told him about Matt, which makes her wonder what she might have said about him, and Dylan in relation to him; whether she and Gabe have talked about her before, and if they have what the tone of those conversations might have been, also what words might have been inside them.

We don't talk about your wife, she then says, so my boyfriend seems not a big deal.

Is he? Gabe says.

Is he what?

Not a big deal?

You mean like your marriage is not a thing, she should say, and have Gabe clarify, just for the record, whether a thing is more or less than a big deal, in his mind, or the same. And if Matt is not a big deal and his marriage is not a thing, then what is a big deal, what is a thing and how is this being decided?

How does it work then, between you and Kate? is what she actually says, which contains none of this.

We've been together a long time.

He commits to full eye contact now, as though he believes this to be the most direct kind of answer, rather than fundamentally meaningless. It's simple at least, We've been together a long time. Insofar as time is logically accrued, over time. We have a lot of history, he could have said, which would imply narrative within that time. I love her, he could have said, too.

Things aren't simple, he tries to continue, but—

I get it, she interrupts, willing him to stop now, requiring this before new things are said like, I love her, for example, already a painful memory, this thing he hasn't said, more powerful than anything he has actually said, or might still say. She'd considered saying those exact words a few nights ago, watching Gabe wipe the sweat off his back after sex, using his gig shirt, which had turned her stomach at the time, but also brought the feeling on, of maybe-love. And partly to see what words like those, from her, might do to the space between them, around them, the space beyond the room. To see if she has influence over any of these things, in any way.

Now she places her hand on his hand and wonders about his age, for some reason, as she runs a finger over the hairs there, as though years might be counted in this way, like rings in a tree. The sensation seems to relax him, which relaxes her. They are relaxed together, for a moment, smug almost, that they have

145

apparently managed to deal with something complex simply by raising and dismissing it.

The main door opens and a large group piles in, shakes out their jackets, settles at the table below the window.

Gabe motions for another beer.

I hear Matt's in Femtech, he then says, makes himself laugh saying, which makes her laugh, not just because it's impressive Matt managed to communicate this fact in the two minutes it took him to carry Kate's bag to her apartment.

What can I say, he's working on some groundbreaking stuff.

Like what?

Fertility app, at the moment.

Okay.

You can basically order a child.

Like, I'll take two in hunter green?

Pretty much.

How about it? Gabe says and pulls a phone from his bag. Not the flip phone she's used to, that's sitting on the bar, but a monster smartphone that makes no sense in his hands.

How many phones do you have?

This one's just for ordering babies.

Gabe points the screen at her, like show me what I'm looking for, when a hand reaches in and intercepts it. Ezra, rescuing them from the curious space they've got into, fake ordering a baby on a Tuesday night. He returns the phone when he finds nothing of interest.

Got to get downstairs anyways, he says, check no one's having sex without me.

He doesn't even pretend to do this, sits before he's finished speaking.

Hazel's on the move, he adds, nodding in the direction of the restroom staircase, where an elderly lady is executing the opposite of a showgirl entrance, ascending slowly, stick first. People seem to know not to help her, even as she stops, twice, takes a breather, starts up again. At the bar, she lifts a brown paper bag, meaning for Gabe and Dylan to part, which they do, despite the fact there are open stools on either side of them. She hooks her stick onto the edge of the bar then drops the bag beside it, *pastrami Reuben, no pickle*, in black marker on the side.

I keep telling her she can get her sandwich delivered, Ezra says.

Why d'you say it like that? says Hazel.

Like what?

Like *sang*wich.

She steps onto the foot rail, edges back onto her stool.

Anyways, the M11 takes me as far as Thirty-Fourth. And they let me buy individuals at the newsstand up there.

She takes a cigarette out of her coat pocket and places it next to the brown bag.

I quit, she says.

How's the Reuben? Gabe asks.

Hazel unwraps it slowly, burlesquely, a pink cliff face between slices of rye.

Gabe nods his approval.

I'm off meat, says Ezra. The *sang*wich kind.

He looks bored as he says this, sick of his own material.

Nate says it takes fifty showers to make one sausage, he goes on.

147

What does that mean, Hazel says, rewrapping her Reuben—it takes fifty showers to make a sausage?

That's how much water.

After a pause.

Wait, two sausages. It takes fifty showers to make two sausages. For twenty-nine years we've been on meat, then they put Nate on this heart health diet, and he likes to make out it's the planet he's saving. So, everyone's off meat.

It's twenty-nine? Gabe says.

He is naturally impressed by this accrual of time.

Gee whizz, Hazel says, deadpan. What's your secret?

He doesn't care how I spend my days, says Ezra. Or with who. Also, I wake him up with a blowjob every morning.

Gabe shoots a look at Dylan, like, how about it?

This manages to feel heavy with romance.

Is he here tonight? she asks, mostly so Gabe will have to address the question of who she is, why she's here.

Jesus, no, says Ezra, you won't find him here. He has wine with dinner.

Gabe laughs and starts up a conversation with Ezra, to his right. Only Dylan is interested in the question of who she is, why she's here.

Hazel skims a handful of corn nuts onto the bar.

You don't want the ones from the top, she says, then takes another handful and slowly rotates towards Dylan.

Abe and I never married, she says, as though they're picking up where they left off, sometime, whenever. Abraham Tempest

III—can you imagine? I used to kid I was in it just for the name, but you've got to be wary of the numeral guys. Right out of the gate you know you're a few versions off the real thing.

She tips the corn nuts into her mouth and glances back at the bowl she's rotated past. Dylan reaches over and slides them closer.

He was a good one, though, Hazel goes on, only he used to buy me these red lipsticks I'd never wear. Tried calling me red too, at the start, like he had something in mind. Got over the red thing real quick but kept going with the lipsticks till he passed. Liked giving them to me, I guess, which I'd go along with, didn't mind, as he was pretty tight about most things . . . a tight guy. Used to divide his Kleenex in two, like so—

She recreates this image in sweeping movements up and outwards from a central point in her lap.

—I came back from the bodega with three-ply once, which nearly did for him. Of all that's too much about this city, it's three-ply pushes him over the edge.

She stops with her hands still in the air, fingers pinched, as if one ply in each, no way to accommodate a third. Then she's back at the corn nuts, explaining how they met in one of the social clubs run out of townhouse basements in Brooklyn, full of young commies, she's saying, as Gabe's face becomes visible again, over her right shoulder, standing now, to make space for Ezra, also the pianist, on another break, and the barman, on the wrong side of the bar, a few younger guys crowding him too, finding any excuse to lean in, it seems like. Gabe's expression has all the hallmarks of a frown, but the energy behind it is a blushing kind of energy, a sort of macho coyness. Is this why he comes? It occurs to her only now how objectively attractive he is, seen from a slight distance, how his appeal is not something she has found out in him, rather that he is simply well made, a well-made man. Disappointing, for some reason.

There's heckling again, from over by the piano, then something cold in her hand, Hazel standing, pressing it into place, saying she has things in the dryer on Bedford. She slides her Reuben from the bar, unhooks her stick, then lowers her head as she crosses the room, as if to become more aerodynamic. There's quite a crowd now, which starts up in unison when the pianist takes his seat again, something from *Sunday in the Park with George* this time—watery, lulling;

Changing, it keeps changing. I see towers where there were trees . . .

The words float up and out onto Grove, as the door opens for Hazel, mingling with the traffic noise in a way that's so on the nose it's almost comical, and yet the mood in the bar is distinctly non ironic.

It's a lipstick Hazel's pressed into her hand.

Tarnished metal, thick deco grooves, like a spent bullet casing. Inside, it's unused, bright red still, with that old-school lipstick smell, weak but distinctive in a way that says it used to be stronger. The smell of missing her mother; that swallowed-marble feeling of watching her dress to go out, pull on the red coat that meant late home, eyes wide in the dark then, waiting for the sound of gravel under tyres, that slow creak outside the bedroom door, and—finally—her mother leaning over, necklace cold from being outside, brushing her face, settling on her cheek or chest.

Have you been misbehaving?

She opens her eyes.

Have you?

Gabe, leaning across Hazel's empty stool.

I feel like you have, he says, close to her face now.

She winds the lipstick back into its case. She would urgently like to be inside the thing which happens next.

Shall we? he says.

Misbehave, he must mean, and she's already off the bar stool, walking ahead of him, not even sure what's downstairs, beyond the toilets she's been warned not to use. Both restrooms are occupied, so they have to wait outside in the strip lighting, low buzz of the ice chest, bowl of NYC condoms on a chair beside it, like mints at a bank. The mood is glitchy, for a moment, strip lit this way, which seems to increase Gabe's sense of urgency, so that when one door opens, he takes her hand and walks her straight in, knocking the shoulder of the guy on his way out. Inside smells of equal parts cleaner and urine, as though the cleaner is urine scented, also something else acrid, like dried vomit from the night before, though there's nothing visible, nowhere to hang anything either, so she drops her bag onto the floor and into whatever. There's a moment of stillness then, in which she's struck by a wave of wanting, not to be fucked by Gabe, but to show herself to him, hold her dress up like a girl in a school yard. He steps towards her and lifts it himself, gathers it against her thigh while he moves his other hand to her hip, and pulls her closer, leans in like he's going to tell her something, instead of just breathing stormwind sounds into her ear, shuffling her backwards, as far

151

as the wall, where he turns her around, gently, in an asking kind of way, and she moves with him, instinctively parting her hands, balancing her forehead against the stone, aware of how she must look from behind, flattened out, neck wrenched left. She's on her own then, for a moment, can sense him a few steps back, taking her in, before the whole of him is up against her, and she's willingly back onto her cheek, also nowhere, when he slows, then quickens, because he is vanishing her, and she is abdicating. Both things together.

Afterwards, she scoops her bag off the floor and wipes it gesturally with the sleeve of her sweater. Gabe pisses, which he's not done in front of her before. The tiled floor amplifies the sound, like a full bucket being emptied into the room, and suddenly they're both laughing, at this, or the thing they've just been complicit in. If they've crossed a line, it's hard to say what kind. What was on the one side, what's on the other.

Gabe zips his fly, rolls his shirtsleeves down and has one arm into his jacket when—

You're bleeding, he says.

She touches her head first, scans her arms, then registers the dark patch on her dress, warped looking, like a cell dividing among printed flowers. There's pain too, the mild, satisfying kind, from a graze on her hip. She dabs at it with toilet roll until Gabe takes over, apologising. He'd been gentle, she reassures him, it had honestly been fine.

Just fine?

They trace the wound back to a rough patch of plaster she'd been pressed against—sharp, raised peaks of some kind of filler.

Ezra's glory hole?

Gorged for her penislessness, she concludes.

Improper use of the venue, Gabe agrees, holding her waist as they head back to the bar, now filled with bodies and something shouty from *Les Mis*.

Only the greats? she says.

Gabe grins and steers her towards the exit.

Ezra's back by the piano, opening and closing his mouth, vaguely in time with the music, not even pretending to form real words. As they pass him, he's reflected in the mirrored mural, for a split second magnificent there, merged with revolutionary flags, fairy-light bursts, top-shelf liquors. The song breaks into parts and quickly collapses, but Ezra continues to open and close his mouth like a cartoon goldfish, as other conversations resume, by panelled walls, under sprouting lamps, *rhubarb, rhubarb*.

At street level, Gabe holds the door for her, chivalrous in a way that is not compatible with the thing they've just been doing. On the sidewalk, he produces her coat, which feels heavy going on, forces her forward, so that she has to take a few steps, a few more, before she drops her head and whatever she's been holding down comes up repeatedly, or continuously, onto the asphalt. Also the rack of weeklies. She only had the one drink, but still feels the need to apologise as she steadies herself and takes a breath. Gabe pulls her hair back when she bends over a second time, brushing her neck with his fingers in a way that manages to turn her on despite what's shooting out of her.

Another hand, then, on her right shoulder.

Another voice.

Jesus, are you okay?

The weight of her coat is cosmic feeling as she straightens up to find Addie standing beside her in a short, black dress and too much eyeliner. She starts to speak, or is already speaking at high speed, asking does she need a cab, water, help getting home. Her speech slows as she takes in the bigger picture: Gabe, with one hand on the small of Dylan's back, the other picking wet hair from her cheek.

She stops.

Oh, she says.

Dylan lifts her skirt.

I cut myself in the bar, I think, she says, as though blood is the thing Addie's noticing, which needs explaining.

Right, says Addie.

I'll find some water, Gabe says.

He nods a hey in Addie's direction, then heads to the bodega.

Hey, Addie says, into the space he leaves behind.

After this, there is quiet.

She's not seen Addie since Sag and feels compelled to apologise again, in person, for the weekend, but there's something new to apologise for already, she can sense, burgeoning here. Some new way she is letting Addie down in this moment. She waits for the admonishment to begin, but nothing comes, and Gabe is getting water, and she has emptied out whatever was in, and perhaps complexity will raise and dismiss itself, again, as it is becoming clear complexity can. This seems unlikely. There's a madness to Addie, of late. A definite madness, she thinks, standing in her own puke, thinking about the sex she's just had, that she can imagine herself saying was the best sex of her life, though she hadn't come, and cannot say whether she was wholly present. She studies Addie's face for signs of having found her out, perversely willing them to appear, so she can ask her what it is she's found, then, crucially, what thing it is replacing. What picture Addie has made of her that she is trapped inside.

You don't have to wait with me, she says.

Addie's mouth opens, just slightly, then fixes itself into an expression Dylan hasn't seen before. Not disapproval, nor disappointment, but pity. Addie pities her. Quite obvious, suddenly, how favourably she's been cropped until now. Hung high, kept safe in this respect.

A bird animates, in a loud rattle of wings from a fire escape on the other side of Grove, and they jump, together, and turn to look at the exact moment a girl walks through the glass storefront opposite. Straight through the glass and onto the street. It seems, for a second, as though maybe this isn't what has happened, as there's no obvious moment of impact, before the shattering glass, the girl carrying on down the block, barely registering, as though it were the most natural thing in the world to exit a room in this way. Stranger still is the fact there is no one with her, rushing to her aid, no concerned friend or bystander, no obvious response at all from inside the structure she has blown open. Just shattering, then silence.

Her walking down the block alone.

PART TWO

Fifteen

Lately there's been crying.

Only at night, but most nights, usually, at some point before sleep. She might be halfway through brushing her teeth when the tears show up, as part of the swoosh and spit of things, or she'll discover them later, wetting a collar, corner of pillow, page of a book. The experience usually lasts a few minutes, which seems long, when you try to imagine crying from a place of non crying, but it's well below average, Wikipedia says—for a woman.

Women tend to cry for about six minutes, where men cry for between two and four.

Featured images:

A two-year-old girl crying

Two women weep at a funeral

A new-born child crying

When a man appears, he is French and shedding tears of patriotic grief—in 1941. This seems like a joke, when it comes. After the Frenchman, there's a diagram of the Lacrimal System, which looks like one half of a pair of opera glasses with fringing and a mountain range and little clouds on stalks. Dali-esque, she thinks, unable then to picture anything Dali. When she Googles him it's like of course she can picture a Dali. In the second row of images there's a massive eye with mountains and clouds behind it, and maybe she was thinking of this exact painting. There is a lone swan too, in a lake, coming out of a tear duct, with a large egg at the end of it—in the Dali.

Women also cry more often than men, Wikipedia says, but not until adolescence. There is no difference at all between the sexes re: crying, until adolescence. That Wikipedia knows of. By adolescence, then, girls have understood their permission to cry, that crying is the expectation, and girls lean in? Or else tears come with the beginning of ritual pain, the breaking down inside, month after month, healing over and over in order to remain, above all, hospitable. Above all, a place where others can grow.

And so, tears.

Lakes of tears with giant eggs at the end of them.

Lacrimation seems like the best description of what's happening to her each night, if she has understood correctly, being the shedding of tears, which are neither emotional nor associated with eye-irritation. This kind of crying has a different chemical make-up to emotional crying, which is a kind of crying that reduces sexual arousal in men. Specifically, emotional tears in women reduce sexual arousal in men. The article does not offer a view on what emotional tears in men do to a woman's arousal, meaning men must not cry such tears, or such tears do nothing to a woman's arousal, or a woman's arousal is irrelevant.

Wikipedia says that Darwin said some zookeepers said that

elephants cry emotional tears. You'd think it would be hard for an elephant to become more likeable. Then you find out it can cry emotional tears.

It's possible, she infers, that her tears could be a delayed reaction to some birth trauma. Her birth had been traumatic, her father says, for him, though her mother rarely speaks on the topic. Forty-eight hours of labour, and tools, he says, meaning forceps, before she was silver-served to the world—bloodied, yellow, soundless. Regardless, she should understand that her crying is only crying, not sobbing, which is accompanied by muscular tremor. This is not her experience, just a steady stream of water coming from her eyes, along with a pressure in her chest, the two connected via a jagged kind of breathing. These things seem to work in an efficient closed circuit, so that the rest of her body, not subject to tremors, is free to make bed, brush teeth, carry on as normal, while tears drip from cheeks and chin.

Epiphora, this is called:

An overflow of tears onto the face

Isn't this all crying? Or, at any moment, might others be crying efficiently and therefore invisibly, draining tears through their nose? Would we know if they were? If we were? In a sub-link now, off tears, or a link within tears, coming off eyelid, it explains that cocaine in the eye inhibits the reflex to cry. Unclear, what set of circumstances led to this discovery. Nose, gums, eyes, vagina, Sally's tried before, with a guy who went into his jacket for condoms but came out with coke.

bookmark: insufflation

bookmark: rewards pathway

bookmark: pupil empathy

She'll return to these, as is trying early nights to get to early mornings, and lacrimation is surely the thing she was after; a way to frame this new nightly happening, fold it into the normal cycle of things:

Cleanse, exfoliate, lacrimate.

Epiphora, she tries to text herself—

euphoria

euphoria

euphoria

—her phone insists, as though it understands the holiness of crying, its release. Like an orgasm, a sneeze, a scream. These things that come from a place of letting go, of what hardly seems to matter.

Sixteen

She's had to get rid of everything, Addie says.

It wouldn't be everything.

Everything.

Sure, says Dylan. But it wouldn't be everything.

She puts Addie on speaker and continues balling socks into the corner of her suitcase.

Everything has to be bagged, then burnt, says Addie. Nothing else works.

Wouldn't you just burn it if you're burning it?

It's both.

I don't think so.

It's both.

After a silence.

Hey, says Addie.

They've not been in touch since the sidewalk, puke, shattering glass. Three weeks now. Some kind of debt accruing, she senses.

Hey, she replies.

They're probably going to have to move out, Addie continues.

I guess that makes sense, if they have to get rid of everything.

Addie sighs, or breathes in.

Can you imagine what that's like?

She could try to imagine a bagging and burning situation, how it would feel to take a match to her storage unit, which she tends to picture floating beside its home on Water Street, for some reason; the grey cube of it adrift in the East River, ablaze too, in the thought experiment Addie's encouraging, bound for Valhalla. Most of what's outside the cube is laid out in front of her now—jeans, shades, laptop—like a punchline to the idea of necessity, of loss. The red dress, she would miss, if she's honest. The one that hits at just the right part of the thigh so it seems the rest of her leg might carry on at that width instead of broadening, the way it suddenly does, with the sleeve that does the same for her arms. The white sneakers that go with it, and spring detours down that fat part of Tenth where Sixth becomes Fifth, bushes lousy with blossom, the kind you might stick your face into on your morning run, if you morning ran.

Easy enough to attempt this exercise, give Addie the response she's looking for, re: their mutual barely friend with bedbugs.

Did you read that piece in the *Times*? she says.

Which one?

About that woman in Massachusetts . . . her dog.

No.

So, this woman—in Massachusetts—took an overdose and while she was passed out, her dog ate her face. I mean, fully chewed it off. Nose, mouth, chin. Apparently, she woke as it was still happening, was rescued, etc. . . . . I forget how. I guess she was able to make a call. Anyway, He was trying to wake me, is what she said when she was interviewed, and they asked about the dog she'd had for a decade. She said he knew something was wrong and was trying to wake her, he was that loyal. That was her reading of the situation, her big discovery, that she was loved. So now she's on the list for a face transplant, ready to live a long life with a new face and the dog that ate the old one.

Jesus.

I know. Can you imagine?

No, I mean what's with that story?

Oh, she says. Sorry. I thought we were trying to imagine things.

/

Do you have stuff there?

Where?

They're in the Charger again, Gabe leaning way back in the driver's seat like he's watching a movie.

In England, do you have stuff there?

What kind of stuff?

Things. You know, stuff you didn't bring over?

Of course.

So, you thought you'd go back?

Not necessarily. I wasn't thinking anything.

It's hard to remember what she might have been thinking then, about now, but it would have been something.

Most of my stuff's here anyway.

So, New York's home?

Home is where your stuff is, do you mean?

Home is where your stuff is . . . There's no place like stuff

Gabe's grinning, at her, or this idea, which has a kind of grim musicality to it. He's been asking things like the stuff question since they set off for JFK, as though only now he's driving her to the airport does he wonder about this part of her; life in another country, family there, other things too. It strikes her he should have wondered before, given the impressive scope of her wondering about him, but she likes that he's wondering now.

She turns on the air.

I guess, home's my storage unit, if those are your criteria.

Gabe makes a huffing noise.

You have a tonne of stuff.

She's supposed to own a floor-through apartment on Avenue A, she only now remembers, full of stuff, so she can only shrug, let him think so. Maybe she is stuff-heavy, but her things are just scattered, like home is scattered, like she is scattered. I am scattered, she might have tried out on him now, if it didn't feel so much like the two of them were on a pedalo suddenly, Williamsburg waterfront filtering in windscreen-wide, hazy beige-browns set against the hard blue lines of Manhattan, cut like a diamond on the other side of the water. Gabe's long legs bend, then straighten, as they drift through consecutive lights. She pictures the ripples they're leaving behind them, all along Kent, concentric circles spreading outwards, hardening in the concrete. As they turn right onto Calyer, there's a loud click from the silver catch she's been fiddling with on the dash, and the glovebox drops open into her lap, like an airline tray table. She starts to burrow, instinctively pushing her hand past what's visible into the dark scoop of space beyond, reading the shapes there.

Can I help you? Gabe asks, not for the first time interrupting the picture she's trying to build of him with the straightforward fact of his presence.

Gum, she says, for the plane.

Her hand is already clamped around something when Gabe says to try the door, and she pulls out a plasticky disc-shaped thing the size of a dinner plate, cheap silver coating coming off in large flakes.

Gabe reddens.

eBay, he says. It was meant to be . . . not like that.

He swallows.

It's a hubcap. The decorative kind.

He must regret saying the thing about decorative as a deep ridge begins to form just above his nose. She holds the hubcap up over the dashboard, like a sad shedding moon. How wantable, this man, is the intense feeling she then experiences all over her body. Not progressively, but everywhere at once. This might have taken her more by surprise if things between them hadn't started to feel like something over the last few weeks, which they've spent together, mostly, while Kate's been away with family, then back in Marfa. Like dog years, these weeks, Gabe coming up to her place, now, instead of her going down to his, which seems as though it has meaning, though it's hard to say what kind. He'll show up on her fire escape after his run and come straight in, if the door's unlocked, or sit out there and smoke until she notices him. Sometimes she'll leave the door wide open, which gives the day an edge even when she knows he's out, so nothing's going to happen. He'll shower as soon as he arrives, to wash off his run, which tends to fast-track sex and could explain the running.

They take baths together too, have taken a few now.

Tubs he calls them.

You want to take a tub?

Middle of the morning they'll do this, bright skylight finding out all the parts of her, as though she's never been naked before, might never be naked again. He waits for the water to fill to the top, almost, then does this gesture for her to get in, like after you, but she can't quite sit, has to sort of half-float, which is foolish feeling and freeing and made her laugh the first time it happened, before he joined her, like they were sharing a tank, then, part of the same experiment, other bodies in other parts of town a part of it too. Gabe seems comfortable watching her indefinitely, so she has to look away first, up through the frosted skylight, offering only a sense of the thing beyond—the occasional shape moving past; clouds, a bird, something imagined. It had been storm weather at the weekend, roof rain hammering while she found out the soft parts of him with the soles of her feet, and he'd reared up, at one point, onto his knees, steam coming off the water, comically primal, like the moment before one animal does something to another in nature—tear it apart, usually—but he'd only bent forward, lips to her ear, asking tell me what you want, already knowing, anyway, how to make the thing he's doing the thing she wants.

That time with the rain:

You know you're in your prime, he says. Sexually.

Is that the thing you are before you die?

He throws a towel over the armchair at the foot of the tub and sits, cooling off, he says, but watching. Showing too.

I meant it as a compliment, he adds.

She leaves him room to factor himself in, say something about how great the sex is, but she seems to be enjoying herself, he explains, is what he'd meant. A shock of cool air, when he opens the window, just a crack, makes her aware of her body again, unsealed-feeling, always, in hot water. Small breasts formless. Hair frizzing limply. He must knock the plug then, as he gets back in, because they fuck until the bath has fully drained, too far into what's happening to register the cushion of water slipping away, bones against white metal, tinny tap smell like blood in the mouth. She must have been on her knees at one point, she'd realised, days later, pressing lightly, pleasingly, on a patch of purpling skin, recycling something in the sensation. Also, creating something new.

Now Gabe's smoking out of the window while they discuss the funeral—her aunt's *galloping cancer* is how she'd referred to it throughout, which had grated as a description, though a person should be able to describe their cancer however they like. It went at more of a trot for about sixteen months, before suddenly escalating, which then took them all by surprise and they'd felt they hadn't had time for things. What things was unclear, she explains, when Gabe asks, or why there hadn't been time.

I'm reading at the funeral, she says. A poem.

Which one?

'Love (III)'.

He shrugs.

Love bade me welcome, but my soul drew back . . .

He tilts his head, like go on.

It's Herbert. A devotional poem, about all love, though. Feel-ings of unworthiness.

Her hand drifts to the cubby behind the gearstick, where there's a stash of wooden toothpicks in cardboard envelopes, like dive-bar matches. She snaps one off, breathes in its musty menthol.

There are two voices, she says. In the poem. One is God. I haven't worked out how to do him, or her, without sounding like a dick.

God would be the lower voice, they agree, in any conversation.

No accent, says Gabe.

Or Geordie, she counters.

Geordie?

From Newcastle. Always comes out on top in testing. If you have a sketchy offer, or a shitload of terms and conditions, you go with a fast-talking Geordie.

It does not make her feel good to be party to this fact. Apply-ing it to Herbert, to God.

Anyway, she redirects, how much longer do you have the place to yourself?

Kate's back tomorrow, then I'm away for a while.

They're good at a while, he and Kate. Deliberate about being together for it, apart for it. Not accidentally apart, unsuccessfully together, like she and Matt seem to be, mostly, these days. She'd said no to Matt coming to the funeral—not immediate family, she'd said of Maye, though Matt knows she may as well be.

Saying goodbye, Gabe feels for her breast. Slips his cold hand up her sweater in the drop-off area, not in a fleeting, flirty way, but determinedly, like he's trying to start something there by the revolving doors. This makes for a weird energy when one of the airport staff knocks on the window and she has to step out of the car with it still up there, sliding off. Almost in the same moment, it feels like, she's pulling her bag up onto the sidewalk and waving at the back of Gabe's car, already merged with the rest of the traffic, honking as he goes out of sight.

A high, strangled sound.

Seventeen

It's shy.

Sorry?

Your cervix.

Oh. Okay.

You have a shy cervix.

So that's . . . ?

It means your womb is tilted slightly, which makes the cervix that bit harder to reach.

Dr Hirt adjusts the speculum.

Dylan would put her pain at around a seven, at this point, were she to be asked, which is unlikely, as this procedure is routine, for a woman. Also, this kind of pain, which is to say women's pain, more commonly known as discomfort.

It's like a donut with a hole in it, Dr Hirt adds, meaning her cervix, all cervixes presumably. She extends one arm behind her, loosely in the direction of a model of the human body, the kind you can take apart organ by organ. This one is closed up, also stops at the waist, so there's just the idea of a donut; floating, coy, remote.

Dylan makes two fists under her lower back.

This will help with any discomfort, says Dr Hirt, as she inserts a longer speculum.

Any.

Three clicks as the device expands.

Try to relax.

Dylan pictures a donut.

You'll need to relax.

—plain, glazed.

She's being punished for stealing health. A full MOT, the surgery called it, when she called from New York, pretending she was still in England: blood pressure, bloods, smear. She is no longer entitled to these things, to anything at all on the NHS, expatriated as she is, in terms of wellbeing. Only a few months of insurance left in America too, where her cervix may never be found. And so, the deceit, and so the longer speculum.

Inflamed, Dr Hirt announces, when at last the cervix appears.

There's blood, too, when the swab comes out.

Dylan mentions the irregular cells they'd found last time, which had come to nothing.

Dr Hirt drops the swab into a tube, the tube into a bag, then begins to write on a white label, presumably what is known at this point:

inflamed

shy

irregular

It's tempting to ask, while Dr Hirt is noting, whether she

might slip a gloved hand into her brain, too, and feel for what's irregular there.

Is the blood a concern? she says.

Most likely commensurate with age, says Dr Hirt.

She pictures a donut that's been left out for a while.

Unpictures it.

Back in the waiting room, she sits in scooped-out plastic and suppresses the same queasy feeling she always gets in this environment. Its hushed shiftiness rank with the horror of other people's bodies. Their flakings, weepings, secretions. Everyone here for some secret shame, no doubt. Something left to get awful. Preposterous, when you think about it, the idea of two bodies seeking one another out, finding ways to become acceptable. And yet, Gabe's cold hand on her breast, and that grunt when he comes. Shivering boy legs at Coney and tell me what you want.

In room 3B, they draw her blood.

Strange, this seems, and darkly separate, as it leaves her body, filling a second tube, then a third. Strange to feel, when the process is over, that she would like it to go on.

That she has more to give.

At the wake, her small talk is broken.

Red-eye > speculum > service is partly to blame, but the issue is also one of mapping. She has been distinctly mappable, until now, to the people in this room. Also, in general.

What matters to you now? a person wants to know when you depart old territory.

And who?

And why?

Also: How are you? someone is bound to ask again.

Untethered, she is bound to reply.

Uncertain.

Unkind, it occurs to her too, is a thing she is becoming.

It's terribly hard to do, someone now says—with the two voices!

A lady approaching: long cardigan, long skirt, long beads.

The Herbert, she clarifies, settling beside the buffet.

Right, Dylan says. Tricky.

Tricky. I like that. You must be the niece from New York?

The lady adjusts a hair comb, extends a hand.

Dawn, she says—Old Norse.

Hyphenated introductions only, today.

Eddic poetry, Dawn expands.

Also, fornaldarsögur.

Oxford Dons around every corner, colleagues of her late aunt, here to remind her of all she has apparently forgotten. Old Norse, for example, is she meant to have studied? Old English she does remember, phonetically, at least—

Ich eom fiscere

I am a fisherman

And:

Whar kepan thu thyn fishas

Where do you keep your fishes?

Or Middle English, is this?

Hilarious to shout everything, for some reason, in this seminar.

THE BOK ĞENESIS
THE BOK!!!

The guy who puked in their final, she remembers vividly. They'd filed in with the usual fanfare—male students in black tie, female students in the black skirts and white shirts they'd bought for their hometown waitressing jobs and would use for the same hometown waitressing jobs upon graduation—and shortly after they sat, the guy behind her puked. The acrid smell remained throughout her translation of *Sir Gawain and the Green Knight*, who she had standing on his horse at one point, which did not seem like a thing he would do, but there hadn't been time for revision. Too busy being with Ed. Wanting to be with Ed. Thinking about wanting to be with Ed, working on the language they were making, which was a living thing. This gone from her too, if Ed sticks it out in Carthusia, a place she's begun to visualise, in which Carthusians, and Ed, and silence.

Dawn hands her a plate.

Anyway, yours was a wonderful reading, she says. I've tried it myself a few times.

Dylan accepts the plate, also the compliment, though she'd found a version online and reproduced it exactly.

I won't, thank you, Dawn then says to the caterer—Scotch eggs make me paranoid.

I feel as though the egg is hiding, she whispers to Dylan, and takes a sandwich from a tray labelled VEG.

Dylan takes a sandwich from MEAT. A small, white triangle, cold to the touch, the same unnatural cold as the roll in her red-eye breakfast this morning. Cold roll, cold egg, cold cutlery, served on a cold tray just before the loo got stuck on flush; monstrous roar threatening to suck the back few rows into oblivion.

Does the shit just go into the air? the kid next to her said.

With all the tissue and piss and stuff?

His mother:

Don't say shit. Don't say piss.

She'd found herself imagining all three of them, then, sucked through the lavatory and into wherever. Flying freely with the shit and the piss, minding none of it, just enjoying the expanse.

I find I'm making washing, Dawn is now saying, vis-à-vis the ongoing good weather, and Dylan would urgently like to be elsewhere.

She can see her family on the far side of the room, her brother Drew bent over the tributes book, while his daughter, Cam, pulls at her grandfather's leg and waits for him to dispense a treat, like a tall, tweed vending machine. The treat appears, Drew turns the page and the leg-pulling resumes, so that the three of them seem to be working in a perfect closed circuit—gleaming, impenetrable.

Dylan warms her sandwich and turns back to Dawn.

Does making washing involve dirtying something which is clean, she asks, or cleaning something which is not dirty?

Eighteen

Her mother is still in bed.

Her migraines are the kind that disappear a person completely. They usually last a couple of days, but this is day four and she's still closed up in her room, holy inside it, as she's always seemed to Dylan in this state, and anyway. That is to say, the surest feeling she has is her love for her mother. Like a gong sounding, or something carved in stone, vast and immovable in vaulted space. If it has a colour, it is bright white, too bright to face directly, which would be to allow for a day when her mother is gone, but the love remains. And so she's learned to feel it sideways, send it into nearby space where necessary, like the empty place laid for her tonight; the rolled-up napkin her father has reached out to touch, twice already, giving himself away in this gesture, the guilty secret they share, this love for her mother, which is total. Unfashionable, Sally insists, to feel this way about a mother, especially for a writer, but there's nothing to be done.

Cam is also in bed.

She'd rejected her aunt's offer of a story with a small, raised hand. *Back from New York!* Drew attempts, whenever Dylan passes through town—*Say thank you for the books, sweets, sneakers, remember?*—but Cam does not remember, nor care to, nor know that well her father's sister, who left before she was born. Opening her mouth wide, tonight, and wobbling a loose tooth. Well aware of the effect this has on her aunt, like clapping at a pigeon.

You're not from this house, she's said to her before.

Another time, pulling her hair into a tight ponytail:

You could be better.

Drew is the other place at the table.

I'm wearing Mum's tights, he's now saying, quoting Maye at his wedding, explaining why she seemed to be creeping around the reception.

Maye was five feet eleven, her late mother a full foot shorter.

Her father moves to the stovetop.

If she'd done her doctorate earlier, he says, she might have met someone herself.

Dylan snorts.

She said so herself, he doubles down, though he has four sisters and often attributes something one has said to the other. Growing up, he'd kept his head down re: sisters, usually accused of being incendiary when he did not.

Henry, you're being incendiary.

He hates it when Dylan calls him Henry, which she finds impossible to resist.

Of course, she was too tall to get parts, he adds.

Maye definitely did say this, regularly offered it up as the reason she ditched the acting career that came before the doctorate—*too tall, you see*.

Perhaps she was too tall, too late. Perhaps she'd worked out that people like a reason for things. That she hadn't married was a source of great suspicion among her sisters. What is she *up* to, their ongoing stage-whispered concern. Otherwise, Maye maintenance was largely left for Henry, a given he should step in to furnish Christmases, Easters, birthdays. The Birthday Triduum, the latter was dubbed, by her mother, which is when Maye would descend for three days—THE DAY and one day either side—in order that she might be treated to dinners out, exhibitions, breakfast on a tray, and such. During the Triduum, the sisters would call, one by one, having sent cards in advance, to Henry's address, of course, just as they attended yesterday's funeral as his special guests, deeply moved, dispersing quickly before the clean-up.

Henry sits and Dylan passes him a hardback book.

I managed to grab you a copy.

Ah, good. Mine's gone wandering.

You mentioned.

There had been much discussion about the book during the wake, Maye's contribution to Beckett studies, her tours performing the one-woman plays: *Rockabye*, *Footfalls*, *Happy Days*. Seated, pacing, buried to the neck. Made for an actress too tall for parts.

Drew leaves to check on Cam, now calling from upstairs.

I'd forgotten she did that.

Henry pauses at the first page of Maye's book.

Did what?

'To Mum'.

Oh.

They didn't get on, you know.

Maye and Gran?

Mother was quite cold, he says—to Maye. Sensed she wanted something from her, I think, which she then resisted.

Dylan's grandmother died when she was five, preserved since then in a series of snapshots: sitting on the edge of a mustard-coloured armchair, waiting to be offered whatever snacks she's laid on—*You'll notice there are eats*; laughing at something her son has said; in a pilling pink dressing gown, stirring Ready Brek; pricking sausages with a small, silver fork. Though vivid, these images are flat, impossible to unpick.

What kind of thing?

Hard to tell, Henry says.

The way he makes a performance of turning the next page makes it seem as though it was not, actually, hard to tell.

I think she found your relationship with your mother quite troubling.

Gran?

Maye.

Troubling how?

You know, hard to accept.

He looks at the book, not at her, as he says this.

In what way? she'd press, if she didn't sense the two of them skating close to some sort of bone.

Does 1983 mean anything to you? she asks instead.

Why?

It's a bit weird, but . . .

She reaches into her bag then slides a small cellophane envelope across the table. Inside this is a lock of hair clipped to a small square of paper, 1983 written on it in black ink.

Henry traps it under his index finger.

Maye's, is it?

Obviously, no?

The hair is clearly Maye's distinctive red. She'd found a whole shoebox filled with such locks, she explains, each in its own envelope, dated, stapled, greying right up until last year.

Where? Henry asks.

On top of her wardrobe.

I see.

Henry had not been allowed to enter Maye's bedroom while she was alive, and must have thought it incendiary to do so now.

There's one for every year, Dylan says, give or take, starting from 1983. I wondered if that year meant anything?

Henry removes his finger from the envelope.

Mother died in '83.

They're quiet for a while, trying to join the dots, which are not easy to join, or comfortable, for some reason. Not the vanity project Dylan assumed, then, Maye recording her precious fading red. In 1983, her mother died and she began to keep locks of her own hair. Storing them as a mother might? Mothering the thing Gran had resisted, a renewed desire for its trappings triggered by her passing? Might there be other things like this—saved paintings, saved poems, a matchbox of teeth? Too late for milk, but whatever darkened molars had latterly given themselves up, rescued, restored, secreted by Maye.

'To Mum', Henry repeats.

His own published works in advanced mathematics are all dedicated to his wife, who laughs each time this happens.

Jesus, is that hair?

Drew bowls back in, and fills all four sections of the toaster.

Cam okay? Henry deflects.

He slips the envelope into the book, like a macabre pressing.

Fine, says Drew. Non-sleeping. At least as bad as the baby.

The baby is in Manchester with her mother Ling.

The baby is bald in a way that is total.

Aren't all babies bald? Sally said.

Dylan showed her a picture.

Shit, she then said. That's a bald baby.

Ling's sister is adamant she has to stop after this one, Drew goes on. She's one of those people who talk about motherhood like it's a conspiracy theory.

Isn't it? says Dylan.

I think we can agree it's an animal instinct.

Oh, good. That's a relief.

I just mean a survival thing, at its root.

So if you don't want a baby you don't want to survive?

Clearly.

Drew laughs and tosses her a piece of toast. Henry insisted on cooking, but it's been nearly two hours and his casserole is yet to materialise. He's currently removing pieces of chicken from the sauce, then splitting the sauce into pans on different heats.

Do you have a plan for the books? he says.

He's referring to the three boxes Dylan's taken from Maye's flat, many of which she already owns in different editions.

Not as yet, she says.

Only now does it occur to her that she has no official shelf, or cupboard, or drawer on either side of the ocean.

It's funny, he adds. Drew was always the reader when you were small.

I'm pretty sure that was me, Dad.

I'd have to confiscate his torch every night.

That was me, Dad. My torch.

Dylan glances at Drew, but he's busy with his phone.

You'd be up too, later than your brother, but not reading.

Doing what?

Getting ready.

Getting ready?

You said you were getting ready.

For what?

Henry moves pan two off the heat, continues to stir pan one.

You'd be putting stickers on things. Et cetera.

What things?

Pencil case, notebook. Et cetera.

There's a violence in Henry's Et cetera, being used here to dismiss or disqualify her. We have the same mathematical brain, he's said before, of he and Drew, who runs a successful hedge fund, while Henry is Emeritus Professor of Mathematics at Merton. And yet Drew is words too, and reading, in this memory, while Dylan is pencil case, notebook. Et cetera. Also unemployed, though she's not planning to share this.

You did read a great deal at university, Henry concedes.

Drew puts down his phone.

Do you remember the Chaucer summer, that insane sunburn you got reading *The Fat Wife of Bath*?

It's *The Wife of Bath*.

Not *The Fat Wife of Bath*?

No.

I could have sworn it was *The Fat Wife of Bath*.

Her father laughs out loud at this, he and Drew closing around another common argument; Dylan's wasted summer, other wasted summers spent reading Chaucer under trees, Old Norse too, most likely, fuck knows. Maye would have been her ally, was always her ally in words, while their brothers found them slippery, unpindownable, set against their beloved numbers. They had a monthly Skype, she and Maye, when she first moved to New York, mostly discussing books. Then Maye said she could hear a virus going in and the calls had stopped. *Let me be a warning to you*, she remembers Maye had said on one of these calls. *Let me be an awful warning to you*, Maye had definitely said, though she cannot now recall why. And there was the package, too, propped inside Maye's front door when she arrived this afternoon. A large, padded envelope containing the painting she apparently asked for, or expressed an interest in, long before Maye began the morbid business of putting names on things around her house. Trodden into the carpet, mostly, Maye's intentions, but this one had stuck. And so, today, this piece of Maye addressed to her, sharp corners cutting through the padded brown, sending out a rain of grey.

There had been a story to go with it—something about Paris and a missed train?—but she forgets now, what it was, and why she'd thought to remember her aunt this way, in dark acrylics, black and blue.

Pinched into tiny peaks, so violently.

Nineteen

Her mother is still in bed.

Boiled eggs for lunch, Henry approaching with a slatted spoon. He's wearing the same high-waisted trousers her grandfather used to wear. Same deep cuff she watched him drop an egg into once, retrieve unbroken, present to her with soldiers.

Store or stork? says Drew.

Stork, says Henry, which means the eggs have appeared in the garden. Her mother has a flawless instinct for when the neighbours' chickens have visited, and where they've left the deposits she then collects in the front pocket of the apron she wears for weeding.

Dylan presses her finger into a small mound of salt, then onto her tongue, and thinks of Gabe. That story he told her about how much he hated eggs as a child. How his grandmother, who knew this, sat him down one afternoon, hard boiled an egg then peeled and presented it to him in two halves—one, then the other—not letting him leave until it was finished. He'd been sick in the kitchen sink, again in the garden later, can't even look at an egg now. She can remember quite clearly the feeling of his hand in hers as he recounted this tale, walking the forty odd blocks from Midtown back to his apartment. Clammy, horny New York evening, on their way to do the thing they spent most of the night doing, which now comes back to her in such vivid detail it feels almost perverse to be making a hole in her egg, pushing a finger of toast as far as it will go.

The rest of the day is spent at Maye's, clearing boxes, then Drew and Cam head back to Manchester and she drives Henry to college, where he's giving an 'informal paper' over dinner.

You'll want to stop when the various lights go red, he says.

Then, as they briefly merge with the motorway:

You'll find cars approaching from your right, terribly quickly.

When she turns on the radio, he reminds her about the time Maye had driven the wrong way up the Exeter bypass and her car had to be lifted over the central reservation. She lets him off the hook, as this is a good story. They discuss work, briefly—she lies, feels bad about this—then things that are wrong with America, then things that are wrong with England; the Referendum Bill, for example, which had its second reading this month.

When we sever these ties, we sever ourselves, says Henry.

At college, he thanks then hugs her, bonily, awkwardly, as though making a hoop with his arms. The hoop is as committed as it is ineffectual, and it occurs to her how happy she is to be inside it. She parks up and considers her options. The plan had been *Alice Through the Looking Glass*, at the Ashmolean. She was meant to go with her mother, who read the books to her over and over, when she was small.

Too late! they'd crow. *Too late! Too late!*

Then:

The little girl just could not sleep
her mother would whisper
because her thoughts were far too deep
keep on whispering
The little girl just could not sleep
The little girl just could not sleep

This kind of reverse psychology guaranteed to send her off. A betrayal to go without her mother today, so she settles on Evensong instead. She used to go most nights, as a student, to watch Ed sing—far left, second row—before he'd upped and chosen silence. More noble or more awful because of his beautiful voice? She has a hunch there may be something in it for her still. The soothing call and response of it. Order of service letting her know what will come, and which way to turn. When to sit, and stand, and kneel. On her way, she makes a detour left down Queen's Lane and looks up at what used to be Professor Irwin's window. Retired now, but his imprint remains in gridded glass, which appears to issue the same orange light that used to signal his presence, though it's not six yet, and June. The feeling of the memory of the light, then, is what's making her pleasurably anxious, recalling that time he'd invited her to his home in Headington, and she'd surprised herself by going, looking for something she couldn't put her finger on. Just more. Vague, consuming, more.

The evening had not delivered.

That is to say it ended not long after it began, with Professor Irwin weeping into her lap about how he missed the wife who'd left him, and the daughter he never saw, who was the same age as Dylan. His grief like iron filings to her longing. Everything muddled. How heavy his head had been, is the thing she remembers most, and how, when she'd tried to move, her hand slipped between cushions into something gritty and damp. An old man's sofa, in an old man's home. The limp watercress she'd noticed next, on the tray of snacks he'd put out; foil-wrapped mints on his windowsill. He hadn't resisted her sliding out from under him. Knew he'd broken whatever spell, terminally damaged whatever idea they'd been working on together, but his pain was bigger.

She lifts her collar against the breeze.

Acknowledges and dismisses this ghost of a ghost.

In Magdalen Chapel, she takes her old seat and watches the choir form its three-layer man cake, split down the middle. A tradition she has to be reminded to be enraged about—that there is no equivalent women cake, nor even man–woman cake held in the same regard. A male voice too, telling her when to sit and when to stand. At the bidding of an invisible male god. Male angels propping up the edifice, one atop each pillar, bearing the roof on folded wings, as if they only need synchronise to lift the lid onto bruised Oxford sky—knocked-about feeling this evening, the product of some light roughhousing.

The sense of imminent crisis, she'd forgotten, straight off:

Oh God, make speed to save us
Oh Lord, make haste to help us

When people bow their heads, she thinks of Ed, in Carthusia, making the very same shape. Ed, in Carthusia, receiving his food through a small window. One conversation a week in the monastery courtyard, for Ed, in Carthusia, though she's considered calling him on several occasions.

He remembering his mercy hath holpen his servant Israel

Holpen is a good word.

Can I holp you?

Psalmody, canticles, anthem. A perfect sound from the man cake, then the kind of pin-drop silence that is unavailable in New York City. Though she's only been to church there once, when she and Clark were doing a New York Easter, at her request. The plan had been St Patrick's on Fifth, then the Easter Parade, but the service was ticketed, donors mainly, clerical bouncers on the door. Our Lady of the Limousines, Clark had said, quite loudly, as they turned to leave. Catholic himself, despite the Church's distaste for the way he lives, his parents' distaste for the way he lives. A la carte, he'll usually say, of his faith—clothes and smells, mostly. Old St Patrick's, then, for Easter, doors flung open onto Mulberry and during the sermon a dog walks in. Half orange, half sherbet pink. Size of a cow. A small Hispanic man follows on rollerblades, as far as the altar steps, where he either puts in or takes out something from the collection basket, does a casual 360, then skates back out onto Mulberry. The dog follows, to loud applause.

She projects a neon dog, then applause, into Magdalen Chapel. Maye's coffin, she projects next, draped with a white sheet when they first arrived, handles making little tents in its surface. Are those her feet? asked Cam, which had broken the ice and allowed them all to laugh.

And, *Let me be an awful warning to you.*

Let me be an awful warning to you, Maye had definitely said to her, arranging a hairclip. Or is she adding the hairclip now? She'll remember this later, when she has her feelings about Maye. About other things, too. The choir files out and the organ goes mad, as it always does.

As though desperately trying to keep the rest of them in.

/

Back at the house, flowers have arrived.

For Maye, from Matt.

The first time they met, Maye blushed for the whole visit. The second time wore a jazzy hairclip. Which is the hairclip memory—Maye quite undone by Matt in her tiny drawing room. No longer too tall for the part.

Her shirt is wet now, from the flowers.

Face too, when she touches it.

/

Her mother is still in bed.

Whatever vine usually climbs up to her room has detached itself from the wall and is hanging like loose cable below closed curtains.

Brisk, this morning, in the guest cottage.

Brisk day, brisk walk, brisk cottage . . .

People do say brisk.

Her mother has set things up the way she used to for paying guests: bud vase, tiny kettle, sugars from all over.

Small lamp in lounge needs bulb, the guest book says.

(did not affect our stay)

And:

Challenged ourselves to spot 60 birds.

A great reason to return!

No birds on the table this morning, only slugs face down in seed and hung from balls of fat like limbless pole dancers. One has made it to the window where it moves in two directions, then stops in the shape of a question mark. It hardly matters why. Last night, the harvesters went by, their blue lights bent across her, taking copies. No word from Gabe still. No sleep since New York, it feels like, or barely any. Seventy-two hours it will have been, when she touches down tonight. Crucial hours, to have missed.

At the far end of the garden, at the edge of the field, what looks like a cow is actually Henry, on all fours, doing something to his mower. There used to be cows not crops. As a child, she would watch them stand perfectly still for long stretches, then animate quite suddenly to swat at invisible flies. Only their tails were engaged in the movement, which didn't feel like it came from the cows at all. Freakish, all that stillness and urgency together; made her glad of the fence. Once, the cows broke through. No one had seen it happen, but there they suddenly were, in a shock of white and black through green leaves. She had cried. She sensed a violence had been done.

You need to push forward, Henry says, when she takes over the mower.

I am pushing forward.

You're pushing down.

She exaggerates her forward motion and the mower digs into the ground, chokes, stops. She had not been pushing down, originally, but Henry reaches for the machine, so that they are holding it together, three hands in total, when her mother appears on the path. The shock of her presence makes them blush, and solves them completely.

Then Dylan's arms are full of mother.

We'll do that walk, shall we?

She hands Dylan a red waterproof, musty smell, like a Cornish summer, hood the shape of the peg. It hangs off her like a bedsheet, while her mother's is stretched to its limit, barely able to accommodate the large chest that made her feel so boyish growing up, waiting to take on this woman-shape. The shape of this woman, specifically. Body first, then the rest. No fuss is the migraines rule, so Dylan doesn't mention this as they start across the garden, walking quietly as far as the fence. Once through the gate, it begins to rain a spritzy kind of rain, secondary feeling, as though the bi-product of some more committed water-related event nearby. Too light to land, the droplets hover, drift sideways, and there's too much to say, suddenly.

Apparently, I grind my teeth, is where she starts, and points out where her front tooth has begun to change shape.

Her mother leans in.

You don't want that, darling.

I know.

Have you seen the dentist?

He gave me a mouthguard to wear at night.

What kind?

Covers the front two teeth, with a ledge.

That should sort it.

She got the mouthguard six months ago, but is yet to wear it. This will presumably become apparent in a single, sharpened fang.

Your father has a mouthguard, her mother says.

Dad grinds?

He's had it for years but it comes out, now, while he's sleeping. His teeth have moved, the dentist thinks. He won't pay for another.

They climb over the stile, Dylan first, then her mother. Crossing the stream, she's reminded of the water feature in the nail place on Christopher, which is meant to remind her of a stream but only reminds her of itself.

Also, Dylan says, I'm cheating on Matt.

Her mother stops.

She is about to take her in hand.

I see, she says.

Ideally, she is about to take her in hand.

Why do you think that is?

She stoops to pick a stem of wild garlic.

I'm not sure, says Dylan.

I see, her mother says, again.

She pushes the garlic into her pocket.

Your father thought about it once.

Thought about what?

Sleeping with other people. Well, another person—one other woman, he had in mind.

Dad?

Yes. He asked what I thought.

What did you say?

I said I didn't think it had anything to do with me.

Dad sleeping with another woman?

His desire to do so, yes.

Your husband.

Yes.

How is that nothing to do with you?

His desires are his own business.

Even if they're problematic?

Even if they're problematic. Though I'm not sure his are. Imagine all of your desire tied up in one person, one thing.

She makes the idea sound preposterous, though this is exactly the thing she is to Dylan's father, all of his desire, which is what makes the story so disorienting. More disorienting still is her reaction. So clearly devoted to, yet totally emotionally independent of, a person. Radical, her mother seems, and suddenly unknowable.

She wipes the edge of her boot against the grass, walks on.

Who was the woman?

I didn't ask.

Weren't you curious?

Why would I be curious?

So you gave him permission?

Not explicitly.

Implicitly?

Darling.

It sounds like you gave him permission.

It's not for me to give your father permission to live his life. Still, it went no further. He said he wasn't interested in acting on it. I think he wanted me to be more horrified, to see if I would be. I think he was disappointed it didn't cause more of a stir.

Faintly amused, is how her mother seems, saying this, and Dylan's surprised to feel sorry for Henry. Above them a bright blue strip of sky meets a dark strip of grey, as though there has been some cosmic miscommunication and two different days have been set in motion.

How would the conversation have gone the other way around, Dylan says, do you think? If you'd asked the same question.

She knows the answer, of course, but wants to see if her mother understands how absolutely her father cannot do without her.

It would never happen, her mother says. My desires are quite simple. I'm not searching all the time like your father, like you.

She picks a tall poppy and hands it to Dylan, somehow complete in this gesture, demonstrating her completeness, how she has made Dylan to be complete, and yet she is apparently more like her father: a searcher, grinder, would-be cheater. Actual cheater, in her case.

When you were small, her mother continues, you'd come into our room at night and cough. Wait a moment. Cough. Find the creakiest part of the floor and shift your weight from foot to foot.

What did I want?

You could never explain. You didn't want to get into bed with us or be returned to your own.

She has a vague memory of this, of the shoe rack nearby; of her mother's red slingbacks; of trying to take tissues loudly out of the box. Had she known what she wanted and been afraid to ask? Had the thing she wanted been unreasonable? Her mother offers no theory—this is the whole of her story.

Perhaps you're not yourself at the moment? she suggests.

Or a replica, is her thought then. Able to pass as herself but missing the details that would give her away to an expert. Except she is the expert too, the only one, and somehow unable to clear the whole thing up.

Her mother takes her hand and squeezes, as if to let her know there are other experts.

They walk on quietly.

I did read, didn't I? she says. When I was little.

All the time.

Dad says I was just putting stickers on stuff.

That too, which he loved, by the way.

He did?

He'd come downstairs with your torch then relay in great detail whatever project you had going, how you said you were getting ready. Mystified by you, then and now. Mesmerised.

Dylan touches the grass, which is damp, not wet.

Can we sit?

They do and she puts her head in her mother's lap.

Her mother hums a tune, strokes her hair.

After a while:

Did they give you a glow-in-the-dark box? she says.

Did who?

For the mouthguard. Your father got a glow-in-the-dark box.

Twenty

Is she sure she can't come in?

She's sure.

In that case, had she realised she might be pregnant?

She moves to the back of the coach.

No, she says. She had not.

That's not why she's tired, she adds, never taken seriously on this point.

On the pill, yes.

Same time every day?

More or less.

More or less?

Yes.

It's not always completely effective, Dr Hirt adds, kindly.

Dylan's only half listening as she then goes on to explain 'important things' about the pregnancy, because seven weeks is the thing she says first, which means early May and Sag, and Matt had definitely pulled out. Seven weeks she says first, which is also

Coney, and do you want me to fuck you without a condom and no one pulling out, at any point.

Gabe, then.

Gabe, all the way to Heathrow.

Gabe, still, when the driver stops unloading bags and goes back into the coach. She can see her case in the hold, right there, about halfway back. No reason she shouldn't climb in? Urgent, suddenly, to get to plane, to train, to city, where things are unfolding without her. Or about to unfold. Or need to, now, in earnest.

The space feels good as she crawls in. She continues past her bag—why not?—as far as the back of the hold, which is flimsy sounding, when she knocks on it, like stage scenery. The driver is audible before he is visible, waving his arms as she burrows sideways into bagscape. Cinematic, he looks, in his rectangle of light.

Funny, too, crawling in after her.

Twenty-one

Self-Portrait is a limestone pillar.

Roughly hewn, sloping at the top, as if part of something lopped off or worn away. There is a hole in its chest, lengths of sheetrock stacked inside.

Either side of this cavity:

3   4

chalked onto the stone.
Self-Portrait is in progress then?
Or:

4   3

Self-Portrait is coming down, preparing to reconfigure.
She circles the piece.

3   4
3   4
3   4

Self-Portrait has stalled, most likely.

Fonseca's last piece, the blurb explains, Made in New York or Italy? Something in the sheetrock says New York City, the kind of Downtown development that shoots up then runs out of steam. Marble lobby, fold-out desk.

Aren't we meant to be amongst the Noguchi?

Sally's voice.

Warm weight of her chin dropping onto Dylan's shoulder.

We are.

The invitation had been wonderfully pretentious. An art-book launch *amongst the Noguchi*, hand-delivered by Kate while she was unpacking yesterday.

You should come, she said.

Also:

Gabe's away, so feel free to swing by later, if you like.

Arguably it would have been easier to swing by later than come to Queens today, but the paper invitation felt more straightforward somehow, clearer about what would be involved. She sent Sally a screenshot, insisting she come too, in town for a few days while Dan thrashes it out with his ex—her words, casually delivered.

I feel like I'm interrupting, Sally says.

Interrupting what?

You. Having an experience. With art.

Sally steps back, looks the piece up and down.

Mothering Child? she suggests.

Then again, in a bad Italian accent—*Mothering Child*—arms stretched wide, in a kind of half curtsy. A flawless impression of Alessandro, their guide on vacation last summer. Everything on the tour Mother and Child, apparently, even that macabre statue in Trastavere, the lumpen, black stump of it: *Mothering Child*. Mother-in-child is closer actually, to the way it sounded, as though the mother were trapped inside the infant, or the infant somehow great with its mother.

Dylan manages a smile and wonders where in *Self-Portrait* a child might grow. Somewhere below the chest cavity seems logical. Smash out a second hole, redistribute the sheetrock, dispense with all that excess self quite easily.

So, is *Gabe* here yet? Sally says, like allegedly that's his name.

She filled her in last night, on parts of him, just the fact of him really, also the fact of Kate, mostly to tempt her to come today. She failed to mention his marital status, also the cells she is making with him, also the fact he likely does not know she's coming, may not be coming himself—away, he said he'd be, when she got back from England. Unspecific about where, or why, or when he might return.

I haven't seen him yet.

Ugh.

Sally steers her towards the lobby, where trays of drinks are being circulated.

Here.

Dylan pulls a jar from her bag.

You brought marmalade?

From mum.

To The Noguchi Museum.

When do I ever see you?

To give me marmalade?

No chunks, as requested.

Sally has met her mother a few times. Twice in New York and once for a wedding back in England, which is when the marmalade came out, Sally's mind was blown, and this tradition was born. A pang of jealousy, always, picturing her mother inside a citrus fug, thinking of Sally.

How's she doing anyway?

Dylan pauses.

Her arms are thinner.

Than what?

Than they were.

Oh.

Some silver lining to Sally's motherlessness. The worst having happened already. Never having considered it the worst to begin with. Let off some kind of hook, in this respect.

Anyway, there was an empty 5kg bag of sugar next to three jars of marmalade, so . . .

Sally grins and holds the jar like a baby, briefly, before passing it back to Dylan, along with the clutch she has no interest in carrying.

Dylan puts both in her bag.

I know you said not to ask—

Dan's fine, Sally anticipates. We're fine.

Okay . . .

We had it out and are moving on.

Had it out how?

I had questions, he answered them.

To your satisfaction?

For now.

There's something almost confrontational in the straightforwardness of this logic.

There was a gift at one point, Sally does concede, which I thought was tacky.

What was it?

Not the gift, the idea we were in a gifting situation.

I have to leave the room when people are receiving gifts, says Dylan. It's like when you're eating out and someone's dessert arrives with a sparkler in it and people start clapping or whatever. It's the most depressing thing.

The most?

That or Administrative Professionals Day. 'They are the wizards behind the curtain.' This email that used to go out once a year at work, to celebrate the executive PAs.

Sent out by the people who make them suicidal for the other three hundred and sixty-four, says Sally, and sees away the last of her drink.

She's not noticed Dylan's not drinking, which Dylan herself is only now noticing, wondering what this means, whether she has inadvertently decided something about the thing she's trying not to think about.

Sally surveys the room.

Amongst your own at last, she says drily.

Makers, she means, creative people. People who like to be adjacent to such people. Everyone here is awful, she's already concluded, but she's jealous, nonetheless. Not of the awfulness, but how unaware of it they appear to be. She's awful too, of course, but knows it, could not fail to know it, as she scans the lobby for Gabe, finding Kate instead, just visible in the far right corner of the room. Black shirt tucked into black harem pants, hair loosely gathered in a gold clip.

The girlfriend?

Sally, following her gaze.

Right.

Pencil skirt?

Pants.

Sally tilts her head.

Huh.

Hot, she means, Kate pulling off harem pants with none of the full-nappy energy that usually follows people around in this look. Luminous, too, her sliver of face, visible in profile, which is the thing Dylan's supposed to be, imminently, or at some point, though wan is the word Sally used to described her on FaceTime last night. Tweakery too, the lobby mirror confirms, strung-out-looking inside its gilded frame.

Can we assume there's no smoking amongst the Noguchi? Sally then says, already headed for the nearest exit.

Dylan shrugs and watches the crowd begin to drift up the main stairs, where it's just been announced a short film is about to roll. She drifts with them, briefly, then peels off left into the ground-floor exhibition, a large, airy space dotted with giant marble sculptures. The most prominent of these looks like a skinny, pink bagel or donut attached to a vertical rod. Distinctly cervical.

Sun at Noon, it is called.

Noguchi would not have known to think of a cervix.

Is unlikely ever to have thought of a cervix.

A small sign says she's not to touch, understanding how tempting to stick an arm through the cervix-sun. A head, a leg. To force one's whole body through its negative space. Her strong instinct is to hug one side of it, push it over, see what it would take to detach it from its metal spine. Or to roll off a sock and press the palm of her foot against its cold marble. There's the thought of Gabe's hand again, then, cold on her breast at JFK. Perhaps he'd shown up already, seen her, and left. Perhaps he could sense from a distance how their collaboration has sprung footnotes, the two of them working with cells now.

In her peripheral vision, she can see Sally, on the other side of the large windows, waving her over. When she gets outside, Kate is standing beside her, leaning in for a light.

I found your friend, she says.

Sally makes an 'I'm finding things out' face with an archness that makes either Kate or Dylan seem ridiculous.

Clients were a no-show, Kate continues—thankfully. Have you had a look around?

Barely, says Dylan, which is a lie.

I found her in front of the parts bin out back, Sally says.

Kate laughs.

The Fonseca? So good. Here for another month.

How do you even move a thing like that? Sally asks, then quickly zones out when Kate starts up on special types of freight, securities, insurance.

But there's always the risk you might destroy something

unrepeatable, says Dylan, thinking of the sheetrock, specifically, its choreographed chaos.

As in, fundamentally change it in some small way.

Yes, there's always that risk.

All so we might be amongst a Fonseca, says Sally.

Kate immediately gets the joke. She hadn't created the invitation, of course, only extended it.

Exactly, she says.

I prefer the miracle shit, Sally adds, and points her cigarette at the piece on the nearby exhibition poster. More sleek, pink, marble, this time as though squirted from a tube, like a worm casting, or a turd, sure, at a stretch.

Why miracle? says Dylan.

You know the kind—flawless, glistening, slides out perfectly whole . . . small push, happy weight of it falling.

Sally is somehow devastating as she builds this image, gold bangles sliding down her tanned arm in a sleek unit.

Also, turns out I shit left, she says.

How? Kate asks.

How do I shit left?

How do you know you shit left?

My boyfriend installed this ridiculous toilet at his place upstate. The neck's much too close to your ass, which means your shit lands on the ledge where it narrows, like it's being served back to you. You can get quite a good look at what's going on, I guess, so there's that, but then you have to kind of nudge it off—I do, at least, with the toilet brush. Anyway, mine always lands left.

My husband can't, Kate says. Shit, that is.

At all? says Sally.

I mean obviously he can make it happen, but it's a challenge.

It occurs to Dylan that Gabe must be in constant physical danger, if this is true. Never not eating.

Sorry, Kate then says, I need to take this.

She drifts off, phone pressed to her ear in a way clearly meant to signal an involved life, in New York, sometimes taking calls. Dylan has one of these too, and takes a call quite often, yet it is not the same thing at all. She continues to observe Kate, over by the tree now, leaning against it, mostly to avoid having to engage with Sally, who is grinning, waiting to discuss any number of things at this point—

Kate is impressive.

Kate said husband.

Something non-Kate.

So, she says, eventually, but Kate's already circling back.

My husband's doing his yearly dog and pony in Hoboken, she says, then explains how his parents throw this anniversary party every year, at the home he grew up in.

It's actually insane, she says. I don't know how to describe it.

The party or the house? Sally asks.

Both, says Kate, and blows a single smoke ring.

He finds their wealth problematic, their displays of it, we both do. But then he also let them buy the apartment for us, so it's like . . .

The one you're in now? Dylan asks, pointlessly.

Yes. It's obviously much more than we need, than anyone

needs. Gabe resisted for a while, then—I don't know what changed.

It helps to focus on Kate's face, at this point, instead of the information leaking from it. The dimple on her right cheek, for example, which is not repeated on her left. The bubblegum pink of her lower lip as she describes how Gabe's dad is a big property guy, was always dismissive of his music, his interests in general.

They have very little in common, she concludes, but Gabe's an only child, like his dad, and there are ties, you know. One of which is showing up at this thing every year, I guess. Thankfully he doesn't make me go.

That Gabe has little in common with his father is good to know. One thing, at least, he's said that's true. Perhaps his dad is also a big guy, which would make it two. Though not a mechanic, evidently, nor living on the other side of the country, with his problem uncle. Who is no uncle at all.

Kate glances at the main entrance. Someone waving her over.

Colleagues, she says, and stubs out her cigarette.

I'm glad you guys came, she adds.

Then:

Don't buy the book.

The last comment is glib, but Kate makes it charming, pulling her hair back into its clip, hooking a thumb under the strap of her bag. They watch her disappear into the building, then Sally helps herself to the bottle of wine she's left on the bench.

I think you can make that work, she says.

What?

Property dynasty. Hoboken.

She makes herself snort saying this.

Seriously, you failed to mention the guy was loaded.

Who tells you they're loaded?

Dylan skips over the extravagant list of fictional things Gabe did mention.

Right, says Sally. Classy guy.

Has the skyline too, she adds.

A running joke about Addie's long-term ex, who used to say this all the time, when hosting on his balcony in Hoboken. As though leaving Manhattan were the only way to actually have it, some kind of hack, rather than the thing a person is forced to do for space, even on his obscene income. Disorienting to imagine Gabe as a teen, looking out from a bigger balcony, wrap-around, plotting riches to rags like some reverse Gatsby.

It's not until they're on the F that Sally brings up:

He's married, then?

She's asking because Kate is likeable. Kate, who until now has been mostly a way to find Gabe out, but emerged today, getting the joke.

And so:

He's married, then?

Yes, she could say, but she doesn't care.

Yes, she could say, but she's proceeding regardless.

Yes, she could say, and there are cells, which Sally would most likely defuse, make practical—just a vial of blood, urine sample, decision to be made still, at this point. She'd be more interested in why Dylan had been lying, to most people, about most things, for some time now. Either way, what's already clear is that the afternoon's discoveries have not diminished her desire to see Gabe, nor her disappointment he's not here this afternoon; this new version already comfortably unspooling alongside the original. His motives for lying might be troubling if she let herself dwell on them, but it's a relief to decide they're not her concern, to be unrigorous in this respect. Most people are lying most of the time, to themselves or someone else.

Yes, she says, eventually. But it's not a thing.

/

On the screen, two paragraphs from yesterday.

Freshly satisfying in focus mode.

A brace.

There had been a third, now relegated to the comments section, where it lives inside a cartoonish speech bubble, floating, tethered to the page by the words:

maybe this?

This chair is part of the problem. Anna's easy chair. No way to take shape in cushions like these, prop laptop, reach lamp— Apollo's creamware torso, his dimmable head.

'Apollo's Torso', of course, is the Rilke.

We could not know his mysterious head . . .

magnificent head?

You must change your life!

The window for writing is closing.

She needs to be writing now, in earnest, and yet there's the question of where in the apartment a cot might go. And, where is the apartment a cot might go? Anna's place hers for another month, the baby, pre-cot, for another seven. If there is to be a baby, a cot, which she cannot think of now, the other thing far more pressing, that she is trying to incubate, and is hard to articulate, but connected to the brace of paragraphs and *maybe this?* Some version of herself that's available only in the words she has not written yet. Which may not reflect her way of seeing when they come. Or else expose it to be ordinary, thin, throwaway.

The chair without cushions could work?

Or the floor, back against the wall?

The wardrobe has potential. Four certain corners, visible joinery, key comically small for an object of this size, she observes, as she opens the door and slots herself inside.

She pulls her laptop onto her knees.

Opens the brace.

BuzzFeed, Reddit.

The brace.

ukhealth.org/pregnancy

ukhealth.org/pregnancy/week-by-week/

Your baby at six weeks, she selects, at random.

is curved and has a tail and looks a bit like a small tadpole

is covered with a thin layer of see-through skin

Thrilling it would have been to know, at six weeks, about the fishlike thing inside her. Whose changeability might have been her changeability? If one can be great with child and great with self. There would be risks, of course, in an arrangement like this. A twin can absorb its sibling, she's read. In some cases, vanish it completely. In other cases, an extra ear, finger, limb will appear where it should not be. Sometimes a tail. These things can be corrected after birth, however. Quite easily removed, the self not brought to term.

She skips ahead—

Your baby at thirteen weeks:
begins to swallow little bits of amniotic fluid
kidneys start to work
fluid passes back as urine

Piss into you, essentially, is what your baby begins to do, at week thirteen.

The *You* section is uneventful:

possible moods, possible cramping, possible breast pain

Business as usual.

At full term, the format changes—*Your Baby* disappears, and there is only *You*, mother merged with child, bizarrely, only after birth. Bound by a stronger invisible chord? Many bad things can happen before this point, also afterwards. People discuss these in forums, ask the same questions over and over, list for one another the same answers.

A question that is missing:

What if the baby arrives healthy, but the mother is stillborn?

/

I have unglued myself from me, Lispector says.

But not how she has done this.

Twenty-two

New Yorker, New York Times.

Bright knives on white side plates.

Gabe, in the kitchen, juicing oranges.

These are perfectly round, and bright, and solid. Just as Gabe is solid, shockingly so, returned to this place where he cuts cleanly through fruit, making halves which are also wholes, complete in themselves, as he is complete in himself, things around him are complete in themselves.

The juicer is chrome, manual, fresh out of the box—*J-J-Juice*, booklet on top—bought by Kate, most likely, for a weekend such as this, now arriving without her. There's wrongness, of course, in the two of them violating her unopened Sunday. Also, a pleasing complicity and the growing sense it might be quite easy to buy into mornings like these. A simple matter of cropping certain desires out, others in. A baby announcement, for example, is made for a crop like this. News about the cells they are making and where they stand, umbilically speaking, which is attached, she's meant to understand, since *Your baby at five weeks.*

She'd planned to share this tomorrow, when they were supposed to meet, but Gabe showed up this morning, swinging a deli bag—

THANK YOU

THANK YOU

THANK YOU

THANK YOU

—saying he's back, and Kate's flown out, and hasn't she left the apartment yet? Not asking her to follow as he headed back down, though assuming she would, which of course she did, down the stairwell, up the gooseneck, into the hole at Coney.

follow, follow, follow

Anything good? he now asks, about the papers, like everything outside the crop is entertainment.

Scars, she says, reading from her phone.

Okay.

Apparently your wounds never really heal. In advanced scurvy they can reopen without warning.

How?

Something to do with vitamin C and collagen production.

Gabe tosses a spent half on the counter.

Anywhere on the body?

Presumably, she says, receptive to the idea that suddenly, unexpectedly, a body might offer up its past. Forgotten, or somehow missed the first time around.

This is news?

I was researching this exhibition.

She opens the paper—

Shots of open pit mining sites, she explains, as she shows Gabe images of whole mountains carved out: one with a hot, white core, like a giant ulcer; another like a ruptured torso, red lake seeping from its middle.

This piece considers the scars they leave on earth.

Jesus, he says.

Then:

Any actual news?

Your Baby at nine weeks seems like actual news, also the things Kate shared amongst the Noguchi, though she can already sense she will say nothing about either this morning, preferring to preserve the delicate balance they are managing to achieve. Of orange halves, orange wholes.

I had this dream the other night, she says. Addie was hosting—the friend you met, sort of, outside the bar. Anyway, it was in Tompkins Square Park, filled with sand, big ditch in the middle . . . only there were no clams, just Addie standing inside the pit, handing up bowls, of her placenta, as it turned out, served from this massive clay pot. And the weird thing was—

That's not the weird thing?

The weird thing was, we were all eating it. We all knew what it was and were eating it anyway.

Your friend's placenta?

Right.

After a pause.

How was it? Gabe says.

Have you had tripe before?

He laughs and hands her a glass of orange juice, lousy with

pulp, like a punchline to the earlier article. There will be no old wounds here, he seems to be saying. All wounds will be new. He pours himself some cereal, tears open the small package that then falls into his bowl. Inside it, a small, plastic dog from some show she hasn't seen: bug-eyed, dayglo blue, monstrous, over-sized tongue hanging left.

He slides it toward her.

I get the toy?

You do.

He opens her hand, kisses a finger.

I don't get along with dogs, he says.

Why's that?

I grew up with them.

And?

They used up all the love in the house.

She's immediately turned on. Not by the sentiment, but the thing Gabe is tempting her to infer. Some beautiful formative pain they will shape together; Gabe's stimulus, her inference, a third thing where there was none. He lets go of her hand, starts shovelling cereal, sucking in milky mouthfuls.

You know, it's basically retardation, he goes on, the thing we mistake for loyalty.

That's nice.

The logical result of domestication.

In dogs? she asks.

It's the dog running the human, in her experience. The human usually far more interested in how the dog is like a human, than how the dog is like itself. A dog knows this, can work with this.

She mentions Clark, who thinks his dog, Jason, is gay.

Why? Gabe asks.

He sleeps with his legs crossed and will only drink Evian.

Gabe barely cracks a smile.

His vague pain is bigger than Jason, the gay dog.

She slips the toy into her pocket and Gabe drops into the easy chair by the window. She opens the *New Yorker*. He opens the *New York Times*. They pass the rest of the morning like this, reading excerpts to one another, Gabe continuing to feed himself, kissing or touching her when he passes in ways that make her begin to consider the crop in earnest, as a likely outcome, weighing what things would come with her and what would stay in storage. Whether it would be simpler to sleep here tonight and just wake up among new things.

After lunch, Gabe naps and she writes, using blue paper she found pinned to the cooler. She tracks the slim, totem shape of the struck-through shopping list on the other side, which forces something poem-like to appear.

What are you doing? Gabe says, when he wakes.

He frowns when she says she's writing, as though he believes her to be rendering him somehow. Validating to think her words might have the power to destabilise him in this way. To destabilise at all. He never asks about her actual book, for which she is grateful.

Gabe swings to his feet.

You want eggs?

I'm amazed you have them, she says.

He stares at her blankly.

Your grandmother . . .

A flicker of recognition—is there?—before:

I'll do you an orange instead, he says, and she lets it go.

He peels then drops the fruit into her upturned palm. She keeps it balanced there, warm and bald and right, as he leaves, then reappears, dropping something onto her side plate.

Burlington 2 Pair Value pack,

Thi Hi

Natural

Reinforced toe

The packaging is a pleasing sulphur yellow—*g* of Burlington looped into a giant teardrop under chunky, black sans serif. The stockinged protagonist, yellow-toned too, looks down her long legs, seemingly at the word DISCONTINUED.

She hadn't forgotten his request.

Would she mind wearing stockings for him some time?

The old kind.

It seemed like he was expecting her to show up with them but she hadn't known what kind were the old kind. That he liked. Now she picks off the round sticker and slides out the piece of card inside. The stockings are thick with a rubberised strip at the top, natural in a way no skin is coloured. They snag when she rolls them on, after showering, which she'd done quite instinctively, sensing something ritualistic about to take place. Gabe does not shower with her, nor help her put the stockings on. The stockings do not change the way he fucks her, whatever fantasy they fulfil playing only in his mind, doing what it's done for him before, or something new each time? At one point, he puts a hand to her breast and begins to squeeze in a way that is strangely perfunctory, as though he's aware of the thing she hasn't yet revealed and is testing this part of her body. The action produces nothing, of course, only the feeling she has every time they fuck, which is that he believes in her body in a way she does not; in bodies in general, but also, specifically, in hers.

He comes first, then moves down her body with his tongue.

He brings her close, then stops and spreads her legs wider.

Nothing, after this.

Just Gabe leaning back, watching, waiting for something to deliver itself—

the fantasy?

the child?

the woman?

She begins to touch herself, relaxes into this, coming hard. Enough to push out a head? A foot? He waits for her breath to slow, then spreads her legs an inch further. Leaves her like this as he goes off to shower.

He doesn't want the stockings back afterwards.

That's not a part of it.

Keep them, he says—enjoy them.

Their balled, nylon spentness at the foot of the bed, like some sad creature has emerged from its sac and crawled out of frame.

Back home, she eats her orange over the sink.

Pins her blue poem to the cooler.

Family Dog

Ate her face, they said,
while she was sleeping.

Loved her so much,
left nothing behind.

trying to save her
(from the dangers of dreaming).

Twenty-three

Amber alert is for a missing kid.

Specifically, a kid that's been abducted.

Happens more than you think, Matt says, as though he imagines this to be the kind of thing people think of, set a mental bar for, who are not opted-in at all times.

I prefer to know, he explained, the first time that noise came out of his phone; date three or four, him hitting golf balls off the roof of Chelsea Piers, her drinking dollar beers from his duffel, skirt blowing up a little, letting it. Then that noise, like something was in the kind of pain that could never be dealt with.

Prefer to know what?

In general, he said, back on his square of fake grass, shifting his weight from one foot to the other for longer than seemed like it could realistically affect the way he hit the ball, which was perfectly, she could tell by the sound, its clean plinkness, and the way it seemed to keep rising over the nets, surely, and on into the Hudson, mingling with what's deeper down. Bodies, apparently, says *New York* magazine, along the city's waterways, bobbing up in April like bloated grey daffodils, signalling spring. Living things, too, mythical sounding; four-foot worms *as big around as your thumb*—razor teeth ready to bring down the FDR Drive, or one of the bridges, or something else, she read, is under threat.

At the surface with Matt, only:

plink—

Life wholly manageable, in that moment. The smallness of that sound, Matt preferring to know in general.

Same date, outside Morandi:

Riverhead, NY . . . Brown Toyota Corolla

Matt reading from the Amber alert, shaking his head; like, who takes a kid?

You wouldn't do it in a brown car, had been her first thought. Too easy to guess at a brown car's wrongness. Slick film along its dash, wheel, lollipop gearstick—round top, pleather scrotum. Receipts for wrong things fused into nooks, where, also, ick and grit and keys to wrong places; the long, loose kind, like you might draw a key. And the kid, of course, wrongest of all, easy to picture in a car that's brown. Knowing or not knowing they've been taken.

Today's alert arrived on their phones together, amber-sounding but no gone kid, just extreme weather:

from 9 p.m. EST
Stay inside

She must have subscribed to the alert by accident, or else you cannot opt out of weather, like a warm pillow strapped to the face, for days now.

Storm watch on CNN, CBS, NBC.

Plans announced, updated, announced again.

The mayor has made them into a pdf.

cc: New York City.

The bird had felt a part of it too, arriving—thrunk—this morning, against the studio window. She'd had time to register it swoop at an angle that would have sent it straight through her forehead, down through her brain, out through her neck, or lodging there, beak parked between the bumps of her spine. She must have seemed like sky to the bird, passable through. A second thrunk, shortly after, though nothing on the sidewalk when Matt went down, not so much as a feather. Weird, he said, as though perhaps he thought it hadn't happened, couldn't have, the way she described.

Now their phones ping in chorus.

Come down whenever.

*******we'll be in****

***

Kate being funny, almost, in this messaging group she has created of she, Dylan and Matt, who in a twist, she bumped into at a tech conference in Chicago.

Everyone else was a weirdo, Matt reported.

How so? she'd said.

Well, it was a tech conference, for a start.

You were there.

This is true.

And so, they are both invited this evening, to *Pam Drinks*, as though the name of the hurricane were the laughable thing about this event. Kate had been carrying cartons of milk up the stairs when she asked them—real, from an animal milk, which no one drinks any more. Too much shit in it, or not enough shit, whichever. Stocking up on essentials, she explained, as though milk were the hygiene factor in an emergency. She'll be producing her own soon, of course, if she chooses. Full of the goodness she apparently has within her. Made by the kind of breasts which will arrive on her body, ready for the emergency that is a child. Which will be an ongoing emergency. A Child Crisis.

Now she makes calls:

Addie, Uptown.

Javi and Clark, in Chelsea.

Sally, upstate, miles from the predicted action.

Zeb, her renter, who sounds like he's ten years old.

We're still in Zone B, Matt announces, when she hangs up.

Optional evacuation, now—in Zone A.

Optional evacuation?

Yes.

Isn't that just leaving?

Matt laughs, then crouches in front of Anna's drinks cabinet.

What would you like me to choose?

She used to wonder a lot about what Matt might choose, that was not her choice, or what he might want, or need, that was not her. It was never other women. She was always the one to notice other women, had to be, denied that basic insecurity so critical in categorising feelings early on, forced to imagine his desire for them in order to feel something like jealousy, to see if she could. The noticing is there with Gabe too, but it works differently. Not wondering what other women might offer that she cannot, but what it is that they might want. Specifically, what it might take to make them come. How do their desires compare to hers?

This looks like the real deal, Matt says, and holds up a bottle of dark crimson liquid—black label, Cyrillic-looking type.

We're not taking that.

Why not?

It's open, for a start.

Everything in here is open.

She turns the bottle in his hand.

Also, that word looks like Secaucus.

Matt disappears, then reappears with two shot glasses.

Prost, he says.

She Prosts back, for some reason sinks the crimson, which tastes like candy-flavoured mouthwash. Also motion sickness. The childhood kind, that moment just after you stop to puke, then go back to your Cherry Coke. She probably shouldn't be drinking until she knows what's what. Not that her body has acknowledged the cells she's making in any way. No sickness since the sidewalk, and the lacrimation has stopped, when arguably it should have increased.

Fine, she says, eventually, to taking the bottle.

Because showing up tonight with open cherry vodka, from Russia or Secaucus, will not be the worst thing she's done to Kate. That much will be obvious, the four of them together.

Kate makes a face like, you realise this is open?

Matt grins then kisses the cheek she's presented in a way that seems almost rehearsed.

Hey, Kate says, and pulls Dylan into a hug.

Gabe is at the kitchen end of the open plan, chopping. He does not look up. They'd agreed to no contact while Matt is here, and Kate is here, and yet he has not been in touch, which feels like it has meaning.

Excuse the decor.

Kate waves a hand at the street-facing windows, each of them crossed, corner to corner, with thick, black tape.

It's meant to stop the glass from blowing in. It probably wouldn't, but there's a storm clause in the home insurance or something.

Are you even insured for acts of God? Matt says.

Acts of man, surely, they can agree at this point, hurricanes in July, though there is something faintly holy about the set-up; the windows' wrong-angled crosses, votives on the ledge below, stick of incense in a pair of white porcelain lips, like some kind of hipster Passover.

Kate shrugs and glances at Gabe, who continues to rock a mezzaluna over something green.

I think we're good, Dylan says, when Matt asks whether they should do upstairs.

She's taking her cue from Anna, who has not been in touch for weeks. Anna, who is unbothered by news of the storm. Anna, who is elsewhere, fucking, making art.

I've got it covered, Gabe says, when Matt then introduces himself and offers a hand in the kitchen.

He redirects Matt after the tray Kate's walking over to the living area; tight parcels of something leaf-wrapped, held together, barely, with cocktail sticks. She leaves the tray on the low coffee table then drifts back to the kitchen, shoeless, sockless, hips barely registering in her leather pencil skirt. At the kitchen counter, she stands beside Gabe and begins layering greenness into a large ceramic bowl. At exactly the moment she is ready for an avocado, Gabe twists one open, removes the stone and passes it sideways. Kate uses a spoon to scoop the flesh onto a chopping slab, then a small knife to slice it lengthways. When she lifts it into the bowl, Gabe is waiting with olive oil and sea salt, to finish.

This choreography is unsettling.

The Millers, making salad.

MILLER G, MILLER K, it now says, down by the buzzers, instead of Apartment Four. Raised white type punched into skinny black tape, by Kate most likely, in an office or a gallery somewhere Downtown. When Matt circles back with a fistful of vine leaves, Dylan takes her chance to move further from The Millers, specifically Gabe being The Millers. She hovers at a console by the central window, where she pretends to consider, then actually considers, a ceramic sculpture she hasn't noticed before. Two smooth blue spheres of different sizes, the smaller coming off the larger, growth-like. The join between them is crude, exaggerated, the clear focus of the piece. *Mothering Child*, she might suggest, if it didn't feel like an announcement.

Have you ever had a bird fly into your windows? she says instead, interrupting whatever conversation has begun in the kitchen.

Kate looks up from her salad.

Sorry?

A bird. Have you ever had one fly into your windows?

Not that I know of. Why?

Two flew into mine this morning.

Two?

Not even the main windows, the smaller one in the study—crashed right into it, one after the other.

Gabe has started off down the hallway. Does he mean her to follow? Nobody thinks it's strange he is yet to address her directly. Apart from her, she thinks it's strange.

Something to do with the storm? Matt suggests.

Could be, says Kate. We're a little low, though. Also, it's usually more of an issue spring and September. Urban glow pulling them off their migration route.

Kate is oddly informed.

Matt thinks I imagined them, says Dylan, watching him swallow another vine leaf.

I didn't say that. I said it was weird there was nothing on the sidewalk.

Someone might have picked them up.

Because people go around picking up birds?

They do, actually, says Kate. I do, anyway, for NYC Audubon, every fall. Collision monitoring, it's called.

She wipes her hand on a dishcloth, picks up her phone.

This is from the financial district, last September.

The two of them look over her shoulder while she scrolls through macabre images of dead birds lined up on brown paper, rows and rows of these, street names and numbers scrawled underneath.

We counted more than three hundred that morning.

Jesus, says Dylan.

Mostly songbirds, Kate adds, zooming into a bright yellow chest, tiny head tucked in, feet curled as if around an imaginary perch.

She tries to picture Kate gathering, cupping, arranging these creatures on parchment. Then pictures Gabe, that moon night, watching Hopper dismember his prey, the way he'd leant in to get at the detail. He's back in the kitchen now, adding minutes to a timer, seasoning something while Kate answers Matt's questions about Audubon.

A big part of it is lobbying, she explains. Mandates for non-reflective building materials, tighter restrictions around urban light at night, that kind of thing . . . The memorial lights are a big one in September—gruesome how many birds get caught up in them. They'll go off for fifteen minutes at a time now, here and there, to give the birds a chance to disperse, but it's a tricky balance, as you can imagine.

Right, Matt says, then pulls himself up onto one of the high bar stools, as though about to sing a ballad.

Kate closes out the bird mausoleum and joins Gabe back on The Millers' side of the counter. Dylan stares over at the bank of windows, mostly to avoid looking at Gabe. Specifically, to avoid his not looking back. There's little evidence of the storm from here, just the stillness of buildings on the other side of Avenue A, high hum of the extractor fan masking whatever wind noise. You'd need to stick your head out to understand the danger, like that girl on the train in Connecticut, was it? Head taken clean off by a branch right before the train station. Or it had come off eventually.

Matt's phone issues another alert, monstrous sounding.

STAY INSIDE NOW

The asterisks are beginning to lose currency. They have no sway with The Millers at all, who have either turned off their phones or found a way to opt out of weather. They're both busy again now, seasoning different pans. Dylan returns Matt's phone, presses her palms into his knees, cups their roundness.

Do they tell you when the child has been found, she asks—when it's an amber alert . . . send another notification or whatever?

I've never had a follow-up, he says.

Perhaps none of them are found.

Kate makes a noise like a laugh, or a cough.

You'd think it'd be red, Dylan continues.

What? says Matt.

The alert, if a kid's been taken.

Amber's the name of a girl.

Oh. Was she found?

I'm not sure.

Matt gives her a look.

Charming dinner party conversation he says, then compliments the vine leaves.

Gabe's speciality, Kate says.

This makes no sense; the intricacy of the folded leaf, Gabe's giant hands, which she can only picture double fisting chilli dogs, corn dogs, deli subs, in a way that manages to seem vital rather than obscene. Matt's appetite has a different energy, like he's one of those kids who's grown up with five siblings and fears missing out. Though it was just him, Adam, his parents, Avery and John. From Michigan. The Michigan Deezers. *We live in Detroit, but we love New York.*

The Deezers love a good vine leaf, Dylan says.

We do, says Matt.

Such an American name, she adds—*Deezer.*

He is American, says Gabe.

Hard not to read something into Gabe's first real contribution, though it is factually accurate.

I don't think there are a tonne of Deezers, Matt adds.

It's more the energy of the word, Dylan says.

That's so American?

Right.

All-American, Matt's dad was, in fact, in something, in college.

Makes you think of a fanny pack, or a leaf blower, she doubles down—a truly American name.

And a truly English name? says Kate.

Makes you wonder whether the person has ever had sex or felt joy.

Even Gabe laughs at this.

Have you? Kate then says.

Had sex?

Felt joy.

Kate means the question to be funny, not intense, which it is, or interesting, which it could be, were they to get into things like, what, actually, is joy? And, what is a normal amount of joy to feel?

Neither, she says. Clearly.

Food's about ten minutes out, Gabe announces, uninterested in her sex having, joy having, anything having, apparently, tonight.

Kate tops everyone up and the group drifts over to the window, where trees along the sidewalk are visible, wrenched left, and a low rumbling sound is clearly audible. They're quiet for a while, watching, listening, as if waiting for the final guest to arrive, the one they all have in common. Or for bird strike, or something else that might challenge the glass, wondering whether the tape would work, willing it to be tested, surely, is the thing they're all doing now.

At the table:

Small forks, green leaves, Gabe's arm moving up Kate's back. Then just below her neck.

Again, a few moments later, working on a loop now.

Kate appears not to notice, or care, as she explains how the vagina is actually the canal leading to the reproductive system and the bit you can see is the vulva.

People misuse both words all the time, she says.

Dylan has been misusing the word vagina but cannot think of a person who uses the word vulva. Certainly not all the time.

Anyway, the book's riveting, Kate goes on.

Gabe makes a face like, no, really, it is, which allows Matt some nervous laughter.

He's actually quite far into his copy, she says.

Gabe has a copy. This is how he knows his way around her in ways she does not. Kate has set the text, and she, Dylan, is the exercise, Gabe's cadaver. Eventually he will take his learnings back to the living body, which is Kate. Or is this happening in parallel?

My cervix is basically impossible to find, she says, feeling the need to correctly name a body part and pleased to have found a way of making this one sound elusive, rather than shy, inflamed, irregular.

I mean, you'll find it eventually, but it takes some effort.

My friend has that, Kate says—retrograde womb?

Retracted, Dylan corrects, delighted.

Tilted, basically, she translates for Matt.

Gabe rocks his chair onto its back legs, as though he senses this part of her tilted towards him, unaware he is in progress there even as they speak, making thin layers of see-through skin. He hovers for a moment, then lands abruptly and looks at her squarely for the first time. He smiles, beamingly, shockingly.

She thinks of asking for a tissue.

You don't have a tissue, do you?

As though the way she asks the question, that he has registered as peculiar before, used as an excuse to lick her, awfully and perfectly, might call up the same impulse. It is not out of the question, suddenly, that Gabe might lean across the table right now, and draw his tongue up her chin.

This does not happen.

Instead, he moves his arm back to Kate's neck, then down between her shoulders, rubbing and gently patting her, as though trying to burp her. As the evening draws on, the room contracts, snaps to the edges of this movement, so that for the next ten minutes—fifteen? twenty?—there's only the sound of distant conversation, Gabe's arm moving in this way.

Tagine passed clockwise.

Dukkah mash.

What's up?

Matt's noticing her untouched food.

I'm not that hungry.

You okay, though?

He nudges her gently.

She has her head in her hands, she realises, is the thing Matt has noticed, elbows on the table, fingers pressed to her temples.

Back's pretty tight again, she says, which is true.

Kate's quickly up then, saying follow me and leading her down the hallway. She finds she's happy to be led like this, by the hand, by Kate, into the bedroom and onto the end of the bed.

Matt made me join him on a run this morning, she says— tweaked something, I guess.

Last-minute survival training? says Kate.

Dylan manufactures a laugh as Kate carries on past her, past the window where naked Gabe has sat, leg hanging down, perfect dick, and she has watched. She pauses at the back wall then presses her hand onto its glossy surface, which springs open like the secret door in a library. She begins to rummage. The longer she does

this, the more obvious it seems that she's about to produce something awful—spent stockings? Dead songbird? Brown Corolla?

Tub of pills, as it turns out. Comedy pop as the lid comes off.

Are you taking anything else?

No.

She did take something before she left, but is also increasingly
open to some kind of alteration.

Kate pours a glass of water from the carafe on the nightstand.

These should sort you out, she says, and drops two capsules
into her hand—one red, one blue.

Take one now. Hit the second later, if you need it.

Which is which?

They're the same, she says.

She shakes the see-through bottle.

I don't know why they come like that.

This could all be some deep mind game, of course: red pill,
blue pill. She swallows red while Kate starts to rub at a tagine
stain on her shirt.

I'm a fucking animal, she says, unbuttoning then walking
over to the bathroom, where she stands in the open doorway
and reveals, in profile, one perfect, upturned breast. She has
meant Dylan to see this, to recognise it as the kind of breast
that is neither too big nor too small for a hand like Gabe's, but a
perfect portion. The kind of breast that is ready, for whatever.
She unhooks a black tee from the back of the door and pulls it
over her head.

Are you sure you don't want a lie-down?

I'm good, says Dylan.

Kate turns around, an immaculate tit-shaped ledge under her gold chain.

What's your side anyway? she says.

My side?

Of the bed.

The question is only strange if Kate does not mean this bed, which of course she does. Of course, Kate knows, would know everything, about how left is her side, when she's here, so Gabe can move easily to the window to smoke, and she can turn to watch, drape the sheet to show only her best flesh.

Both, she says, unblinking.

Kate rests her arm against the doorframe, easy and right inside her womanhood. It occurs to Dylan how much she would like to join her in this state, to be easy and right together, but there is no time, tonight, for this. Everything converging suddenly, so that she must prioritise—leaving, now, for example, if Kate has found her out.

Both?

I can only sleep in a kind of star shape.

That's why you keep Matt on the West Coast, Kate laughs, then tells Dylan how she used to make Gabe sleep on the sofa when they started dating, and perhaps Kate does not know what is happening, and was just making small talk, which is a thing some people do.

Back at the table, Gabe is slicing some kind of chocolate pie.

He looks up from his plate.

Everything okay?

His first direct words to her this evening.

Now would be the time to leave, as planned, but the question comes with eye contact, and she's undone.

Better, thanks.

Gabe's offered to do upstairs, Matt then says, standing.

Do what?

The windows. It's a good idea, I think—do you have the key?

Gabe's up then too, pulling tape and a pair of scissors from the kitchen drawer. He has contrived a way to be with her, briefly, alone.

I'll go, she says. I need a sweater, anyway.

Fair enough.

Matt sits, happy to return to his pie, Kate adding cream.

In the stairwell, Gabe waits for her to go ahead. He stays a few steps behind the whole way up, then passes behind her when she stoops to move the doorstop. He heads straight into the bath-room, where for some reason he begins to wash his hands.

She follows and waits in the doorway.

I take it dinner was Kate's idea?

You think?

Gabe does not look up from the sink.

You could have said no, she says.

I didn't get much of a warning.

Me neither, she lies.

Still, Gabe says, it's weird you came.

It is, she says.

She'd meant this to come out as a question—it is?—though of course it is, weird, that she came.

243

Gabe seems amused at this apparent moment of self-awareness and visibly relaxes.

So, what are the chances we're not getting found out? he says, and jerks a towel off the handrail in a way that makes the stakes seem laughably low, as though there are barely stakes at all.

She presses a fist into her lower back. Slow spasms now, spreading outwards.

Would it be the worst thing? she says, mostly to see what Gabe will say.

He moves the towel slowly, methodically between each finger then brings his right hand to his face and stretches his right eye open. He moves his other hand to his eyeball, then wipes his index finger on the white porcelain. He repeats this with his left eye, then blinks, hands either side of the sink, bracing.

Honey, he says, seemingly to his own reflection.

Honey, he says again, this time pulling her into his chest; fug of drugstore cologne.

He lowers his mouth to her ear.

I have a life, he whispers.

There's a pause before he then moves his hands to her shoulders and shuffles her backwards.

You know how it is.

That he has a life, he means.

A life—ha!

Brutally efficient, cauterising all lines of enquiry.

She can only think to lean towards him, his hands quickly back at her shoulders, moving her three, four steps backwards, this time, then pressing down, as if to fix her in place. *I have a life,*

Gabe has said, whispered, in fact, as though it is a secret he's been keeping. A life inside which he is, and she is not. This is what she's meant to understand by his placing her here in this way—apart.

It's out of my control, he adds.

When he lifts the seat to piss, she's actually turned on, so total is this moment of humiliation, somehow metabolised already into thoughts like how long, realistically, might she have to make something happen before they go back down? And how might this be achieved? There's the issue of her not being able to move from the spot where he has placed her, when she tries, as if his hands are still pressing down, rather than shaking himself off, picking up tape and scissors, walking them past the tub where she has floated and he has watched. She's able to move again, once Gabe's out of sight, though this does not appeal as much as lying down, for example, and waiting for this moment to pass.

There's the blue pill still, in her back pocket.

She drops it onto her tongue and holds her head under the running tap. After she swallows, she presses a fingertip into one of the lenses Gabe has disposed of, just as he is trying to dispose of her. You know how it is. She pinches it between her thumb and forefinger and listens to the violent sound of tape coming off the roll next door. Meant to keep out what, exactly, at this point?

Back in the living room, she lifts Matt's sweatshirt off the armchair then passes quietly behind Gabe, coughing once to make sure she's still able to make a sound, though a scream ought to be next, or a laugh, because Gabe has a life and wasn't she aware? She waits for him, for some reason, opposite the Fontana, understanding instinctively now how he has made the cuts. Swiftly,

245

reflexively hurting the blue. Her head's not quite through the neck of Matt's sweatshirt when Gabe passes, saying, Let's go, and starting down the stairs. She takes the first two steps blind, for a split-second imagining the kind of fall in which she is ended, and Gabe held accountable, but her head pops through and her descent continues unremarkably.

Doesn't it seem boring, she now thinks to say—your life?

But the moment for this has passed, and sorry is what comes out instead, under her breath. It's unclear for what, and thankfully Gabe doesn't hear, as they cross the landing and step back into his apartment, where Matt now sits in the glow of candles. Kate continues to light more, anticipating a power outage yet to happen, or creating the semblance of one, doing her best to throw a good hurricane. The effect on the scene is dreamy, grainy, like a photo taken in low light, when the taker has moved, just slightly, and made a smear of the moment. Gabe enters frame and takes his mark on one of the two large armchairs. Matt is seated on the long, white sofa opposite, where he continues to read from the storm scale, at Kate's request.

Wind felt on face
Umbrellas used with difficulty
Inconvenience walking against wind
Strong Gale, is my guess, says Matt. At the moment.
Kate shakes out the taper.
As opposed to?
Moderate gale, fresh gale, whole gale . . .
What's Hurricane? says Gabe.
Devastation occurs, says Matt.

Excellent, says Kate, then sitting in the second armchair.

What's the opposite—like a one?

Calm, Matt says. *Smoke rises vertically.*

Gabe nods, likes calm, smoke rising vertically.

Gabe, who has a life, and has passed effortlessly into this next scene, its pleasing rhythmic patter, which has the feeling of stage dialogue: *moderate gale, fresh gale, strong gale.*

It's hot in here; don't you think it's hot in here? Dylan then says, ruining this with repetition.

She pulls off Matt's giant sweatshirt.

Didn't you just go up to get that? he says.

I did.

Quaint, at this point, the idea of continuity. Presumably the pill will kick in soon and level her out. Hard to say whether it was ten minutes or ten days ago that she was in the bedroom with Kate, spasms growing deeper now, though at more of a distance—manageable, malleable, somehow, like this evening is beginning to feel, returned to scratch.

Are you sure you're okay? says Matt.

Fine, she says. I'm fine.

Did you see that piece in the *Post*? Kate says. About what a Category Five would do to New York—hurricane, that is, not storm. Bridges flooded, boat seats to the highest bidder. City wiped out for good, basically.

Jesus, says Matt, says Gabe.

Dates passed clockwise.

Stovetop espresso.

The alerts pick up, insist they stay inside.

NOW. NOW!! *NOW****

Disappointing when Pam is then downgraded to Superstorm. Some new trajectory needed for this evening, devastation withheld. Which might be achieved by slipping into the dialogue, tinkering, sending it in a direction? The right form of words will be key, she's thinking, when it occurs to her this is why she'd been sorry on the stairwell, already knowing what she was going to say tonight, since, *I have a life*, or the avocado, for some reason, had been the inciting incident. The way Gabe had passed it sideways, so casually.

She scans the room.

Intensely flesh coloured, Gabe seems, and Kate, and Matt, as she imagines how this new scene might go. Her hand the same vivid pink as she holds onto the coffee table and steadies herself. Kate will be grateful, she can tell. She will be doing Kate a favour, her hurricane gone flat.

My mother likes Bing Crosby, is the thing Kate's saying now, for example.

Correction: *Sometimes*, my mother likes Bing Crosby.

Sometimes? says Matt.

Sometimes she likes him, and sometimes she feels like he should be selling her a second-hand car.

Why?

Something to do with his height and the suits they put him in. How orange he seems, even in black-and-white . . . that snow scene, especially, in *White Christmas*.

I can't say I know the film, says Matt, formal sounding, as though he understands *White Christmas* to be a classic.

There's this freakish scene, Kate continues, with the four of them sat around a table at a diner, singing, pointing at a piece of cardboard with a picture of snow on it, fake-looking snow, manically harmonising the word snow . . . *snow, snow, snow* . . . looking at the board, then each other—pointing, harmonising, looking—like they're pitching an idea that doesn't exist yet.

She sips her espresso.

Bing's selling hardest, she says. Bing's selling his ass off.

This talk of snow, even fake snow, a picture of fake snow, is disorienting, set against the extreme heat Dylan is now feeling. The flame in front of her flickers, struggles, tries to push upwards, though there's no obvious breeze in the apartment, nothing to make it strobe and seize and cause this heat somehow? Or else the many small flames Kate has made are the source of this pressure, building, making her sweat profusely, that all-over, summer kind of sweat, already collected heavily at the back of her thighs.

Kate leans in.

Everything okay?

Dylan shifts in her seat.

Aren't you hot? she says. I feel like it's weirdly hot.

Kate shrugs.

Shall I turn on the air?

The boys look fine, temperate, conversing across the coffee table.

I'll just grab some water, I think.

Kate stands as she stands.

Let me, she says, then drops her eyes and fixes them there.

It takes Dylan a moment to connect her body to the blood,

which is not a small amount of blood, but a severed cock amount of blood, spread as far as mid-thigh on one leg, higher up on the other. It's a stifled laugh that comes out when she does compute, because here is Gabe, and here is Kate, and Matt, and there is blood all over her crotch.

Kate mobilises quickly, grabbing Matt's sweatshirt from the arm of the sofa and wrapping it around her waist, managing to get quite far with this before the boys look over, wondering why all the sudden movement. She remains passive as Kate ties the sleeves behind her back, like a giant apron. Only when the boys stop talking completely, does she look back at the sofa. A broad, uneven patch of red on its textured white, narrowing towards the table, like a map of some hurt country. She must have been bleeding for a while. Unless this is how it comes, all at once, when something like this happens—quite clear, to everyone, what this is.

Shit, Matt says, standing.

She could sit again, try to cover the stain, but her strong sense is that whatever has begun may become terminal if she moves in any way. That the rest of her may rush out too.

She stands still, legs clamped together, holding herself in.

Gabe is the last to notice, eyes wide, shifting back in his chair.

Matt takes a step closer.

What's even . . . ? Are you okay?

She glances behind her again, then back at Kate.

Your sofa, she says.

Fuck the sofa. What do you need?

This is the question, still, even when you're bleeding out.

Get up, Kate says to Gabe. Matt, give me your phone.

I'm honestly fine, says Dylan, I just can't—

Move, is the word she's looking for.

What she needs is to be elsewhere.

She can map her way out in two small journeys; sofa to lamp, lamp to hallway. She will have to separate her legs for this, which may not be possible, blood in one of her sneakers now, trickling down the back of her leg.

Yeah, I should probably go, she then says, matter-of-factly, which puts Matt into overdrive, wrapping his arm around her, sort of half lifting her, as though gravity is the thing that is threatening to her in this moment.

She takes a small step.

Another.

Relaxes her legs when she realises she can, moving quite quickly after this, as far as the lamp, where she pauses, as planned, and takes stock.

I'm going to head off, she repeats, like all that's happening is she's just calling it a night. With this, she moves swiftly through the second leg, at a trot it feels like, into the stairwell. Matt's right behind her, picking up his fallen sweatshirt, trying to wrap it around her shoulders for some reason.

You should let me, he says, but she's already through the open door, down the hallway and into the bathroom, locking herself in.

She kicks off her shoes.

I'm fine, she says, when Matt begins to knock. Really, it's whatever.

She peels off the wetness of her jeans, and breathes. Safely over the toilet, she's able to think for the first time about what is leaking from her, still, palpably. Also, of the scene she's just left. Fled from, in fact. She moves her feet forwards, then backwards, the white whites and blue blues of the tiles set off by the red streaks she's making, as though their creator had exactly this is mind. The amount of blood is stunning, underfoot, on her jeans, coming out of her still. Stunning a person has this much blood to spare. To start with. She is stunned by her body, even as it is failing.

Matt's voice has risen to a shout now, insisting she unlocks the door. There's a second voice too, Kate's—something about an ambulance is on its way. When knocking becomes banging, what she means to do is reassure, let everyone know she'd just like a moment but, I think I need help, is what she hears herself saying.

You need to come in here now.

Twenty-four

A green shoot.

Commotion, and a green shoot pushing up through her abdomen.

Doctors huddle, discuss whether to cut or to pull.

Green is from the natural world, they agree, inclined to pull.

She is meant to feel grateful about how the shoot has arranged itself, missing arteries, organs, etc.

There is no pain, just the idea of pain.

Pain is to be avoided at all costs, a loved one agrees, then shrinks to a tiny vase and fills with green flowers.

Her bleeding had been Category 2.

Or Grade 2, did they say?

Either way, more than twenty per cent of her blood volume gone. Issues with clotting and a burst cyst, the doctor now explains, but also some people just bleed more than others in situations like this, even early on.

No joke, he adds, as though she might be finding something funny.

A blood transfusion, therefore, and a small surgery for the cyst, over the last two days, two nights, during which she's been mostly out of it, according to Addie. Spiked a fever at one point, which concerned them, but passed—

This too shall pass . . .

—her mother's voice through iPhone glass, cool against her hot cheek. Addie conjuring her between sleeps, before visitors, deli platters, updates on damage to the city, which has been modest, all considered, save for a single townhouse on Twenty-Second whose façade slid clean off the building. Rooms opening out onto the block like a giant doll's house.

And Matt, of course.

Both nights on a roll-away bed, which the nurses call a cot, as though Matt is her giant baby. In the morning, the cot is gone, and Matt has moved to a small, plastic chair, saying no need to speak, at first, now listening as she explains as much as she can about the last weeks and months, heart monitor keeping time in the background, punctuating his silence.

Okay, he says, eventually.

Then:

I see.

Entirely like her mother in this response. The parallel hurts her. Because she does not know how to make someone like Matt happy? Because a baby would have made her mother completely happy? They keep talking for most of the morning.

Some things Matt says:

that she is selfish

that he loves her

that she doesn't want to be in a relationship

I'm sorry, she says again, and means again, seeing quite clearly how Matt is kinder as well as better. Rightly looking up to him when she discovers he's packed her up and moved her to Addie's, along with the cat, which he found, eventually, in the shed by the bird bath, along with the rest of Mercury and other half-eaten creatures. Disarticulated, is the word he uses, to describe these things. A good word. The thing she's been looking for—a severing of what's become fixed. To become smoothed over, then, and variable. She does not communicate this to Matt, only says thank you, and that she has loved him, quite deeply, in her way, which has disappointed her too, to discover how inadequate.

His chair seems tiny, when he stands. It's unbearably moving, the size of this chair, relative to Matt, how he then closes the door, gently, as though she is sleeping. Leaving her at risk, too, she senses. Not of falling, but of floating upwards indefinitely.

She becomes rigid, usually, when the nurse arrives to refresh the thing they've been lifting her into, and out of, the last few days, like some mad, incontinent baby. But she finds she's happy to submit to it now, to imagine herself swaddled next, waiting to be picked up by a carer. A full-time carer.

No word from Gabe.

Who has a life, after all.

A life.

No word from Gabe, and Kate still none the wiser, she's thinking, as the nurse walks out, and Kate walks in. Matt gone, Addie off filling in forms and Kate just walks in and begins to speak, in an unfamiliar torrent, at first, so that it takes some time to realise what's happening. Which is an apology.

Kate is apologising.

He has this need for something new, Kate's saying. To feel newness, something like it, which shows up like clockwork. It's easy to see coming, so I'll just put someone in his way, I guess. Make space. You know, for things to happen.

She pauses as if waiting for Dylan to understand what she has done, which is to serve her up, like a vine leaf at one of her shindigs.

People usually get tired of him, she continues, then explains how it's a system which works for them, usually.

Her apology does not include the word sorry, nor seems to be an apology as it unfolds, more of a debrief on how the system has fallen short. Kate come to Dylan's bedside to think aloud about why this might be.

Gabe has some issues, she concludes, eventually. You know . . .

Dylan does not know, nor ask, preferring to remain perfectly still, and silent. As though there might be agency available in this. A certain dignity in wondering but not asking whether Gabe had registered her bleeding out the other night. Whether he's aware of the system, when it's working, or whether that's not how the system works, which, until now, has worked for them—after this blip, might work again.

Kate does not ask whether the blip was Gabe's, nor about the state of Dylan's body, the blip still making its slow exit, only wipes her sunglasses on the sleeve of her jacket. Dylan's strong impulse is to scream, sound an alarm, hit whatever button there's meant to be, in a place like this, isn't there, to have a person removed? But she's exhausted. She closes her eyes instead, and waits for herself to disappear. Like a child who has not quite understood the game of hide-and-seek.

Twenty-five

No sink in the room, no toilet.

Just a smattering of tile on unfinished wall. Fern-filled urns on the wedge-shaped ledge where the roof slopes down. A single jar of bath salts, cork-topped, sweet-shop scoop.

The bath is sunken, oversized. This helps with the thing she's been doing, which is to make herself as small as possible, in her mind's eye; shrink herself into something manageable as she waits for the steam to disappear her, white noise of the fan to lull her deeper into non-ness. Sometimes, she'll throw a leg over the side, or up onto the ledge, feet among the ferns. Sometimes, Sally will join—cushion, book, cigarette—notice tears on her face, which had seemed to her like steam, and it's just my body, she'll explain, when this happens, and Sally will reach out and touch some part of her.

You could have died, Sally says, one time, soft sliver of light spilling under the door.

And she does remember thinking it might be dying, that

feeling like standing up too fast, but over and over. That it was not as bad as you might think. Mostly, Sally leaves her alone to heal, which happens gradually, efficiently, as a woman's body is designed to do. Ongoing cramps, for a while. Tiny aftershocks of the labour that wasn't. Blood in her bathwater, too, for at least a week; then a dull, brown line when she pulls the plug; then nothing.

Only grief.

At the loss of the baby, which is to be expected, and chemical, in part, so out of her control. But also, and more profoundly, at the other loss, which is the idea of the baby. Of any baby. As certain as it is sudden, her realisation a baby is not a thing she wants, nor will ever want.

Crushing, this second grief.

So much so that she begins to rationalise from the body outwards—that she is mourning some part of her womanhood gone missing . . . a fundamental impulse it's dirty not to have . . . but even as she auditions this logic, she understands it's something far more basic and shameful that she's grieving. Which is a thing which happens next. That promise, as a woman, of becoming at some point blissfully incidental in service of a child. Turned squarely away from the self, and solved somehow, in this respect. This, the little death she is feeling now. Gabe, another cauterised escape. An alp of self rising in their stead—its terrifying long shadow. There's another thought, too, that is insane, and she has had before, which is that to be a mother is to have one always around. That mother would be her, of course, so fundamentally compromised. But still.

Stop! Come back! she would say, as a child, her mother right beside her.

I miss you, whilst holding her hand.

How to feel this way about oneself, so wholly bought in? So concerned about oneself gone missing, even for a moment? These are the things she turns over in bath, in bed, on porch swing, while Sally brings iced tea, takeout, instructions for the air con they have failed to fix, Dan gone for July, summer beginning to rage. Sally manages not to laugh when she shares the thing about a mother always around, only shakes out a towel and wipes off the fold-out chairs they've brought out to the pool, which has taken on a certain pond-like quality under her management. She's wearing a crop top and pyjama pants, it looks like, which manage to give off a cruise-wear energy despite the Cliff Bar she's part way through demolishing. The miracle of Sally. Sally, who has sprung a family overnight and just folded it in, the way she does everything, to her round-the-clock hustle.

She shrugs when Dylan says something to this effect.

Mostly I feel like that character in that Lorrie Moore story.

Which one?

Accidentally kills her friend's baby at a family picnic.

Okay.

She's holding the baby, then there's a bee in her face, or a wasp, and she leans onto a rotten picnic table and she and the baby go down. Her on top of the baby . . . or just the baby goes down? Either way, the baby doesn't make it and she basically goes into hiding. Before this happens, people are always telling her she'd be a great mother.

No one has ever said this to you.

This is true.

They laugh at this, then over the course of the afternoon, at everything else that is no joke. Like, *I have a life*, and no word from Gabe, and served up like a vine leaf.

Do you think they're back to setting each other up? Sally asks.

I don't think it works like that.

Like what?

Both ways, I mean. People usually get tired of him was her main point.

Not her?

Apparently.

They watch a bird land in the pool, nose at a floating branch.

Matt thinks I don't want to be in a relationship, she says.

Do you?

I don't want a baby.

You realise these are two different things?

Also, I don't like to fail.

Some kind of Tourette's beginning to take over now. Failure at what, does she mean—at intimacy? Her body? New York? Or more fundamentally, at the proposition of herself, so painstakingly assembled in her twenties, now beginning to glitch.

You could try leaning into it, Sally says, as though it is perfectly clear to her friend how she is failing.

How do you mean?

Have a go at not caring.

What she feels like she needs most, she then tries to explain, is to be able to reject the old certainties, but without looking for new ones, at least for a while. To not skip over the place between the two.

You want to be uncertain? says Sally.

The idea seemed more philosophical in her head.

Yes, I guess. And fine with it.

So be uncertain.

Borderline aggressive, the simplicity of this proposal, and impossible to visualise. Best not to visualise, then. To take time off from manufacturing the future, which will show up anyway, as the future is wont to do.

When Addie arrives at the end of the week, there is home cooking and a trip to the GENERAL STORE. This is the only store and looks a lot like a Harvester—a restaurant chain back home, she explains to Sally, from childhood car journeys, in lay-bys, on roundabouts, is how she remembers a Harvester, though this cannot be right. The main thing was the advert anyway, which seemed to be on all the time, where a lady greets a family and asks, 'Have you ever been to a Harvester before?' That's it. The only thing to know about a Harvester, that this question will come at you, and you'll feel great when it does. Incidental, what might come afterwards.

Did you ever go to a Harvester? Sally then asks, and it does nothing for her.

Back at the house, Addie unpacks groceries while they discuss how her uncertainty might be facilitated, practically speaking. Sally brings up a guy Dan knows, who has a place a few hours west of here. He'll be looking for someone to keep the house running over the winter, apparently. Peppercorn rent, she'd just need to heat the place, take the car out, that kind of thing. She nods, pretends to sound interested, as though she could ever leave the city. Mostly she's watching Addie prep, peel, pre-heat. Clark said she'd throw a good convalescence, which is how he's describing Dylan's time up here, at altitude. Not un-Victorian, he pointed out on their call this morning, during which, also:

Twyla Carp

Wu Tang Clam

Sir Anchovy Hopkins

Addie does throw a good convalescence. Intricately plotted, as the weekend unfolds, in a way that's hard not to admire. How determined she is in her ideas of things, of herself. Gladiatorial, how she will continue, after this weekend, to pair cropped pants with whatever and head into a city that never quite affirms, nor can ever quite deliver. An act of radical hope, Addie's New York.

On the last night, they abandon two movies and by eleven Dylan's in bed, watching the clip she's been watching on and off since the hospital. *Traumatic birth* was the search term that served up this cow, impossible to take your eyes off—calf half in, half out—when she starts to move, too much, too fast, you can sense, before she begins to trot, then canter at some speed from the thing she's trying to birth, so that for a while it seems to hang, and swing in a kind of bubble, before dropping, then dragging behind her. A howl, from the cow, when the farmer enters frame. A bucking kind of jerking when he cuts the chord. No movement from the calf.

Just one broken body responding to another, when she first watched this. Respect, above all, for the honesty of all fours. Now new things reveal themselves, each time she watches:

the elegant curve of the cow's back leg
that dark patch along her flank, like spilt ink
a strange beauty in her awful falsetto
her toss of the head, at the end, blink and you'll miss it—
in pain, but also free.

Twenty-six

Back in the city.

August, like a brick through the window.

All-time, big-time high, says NBC.

Urban heat island, says ABC, then CBS, like it's a reality show they're on, this New York summer. Last one standing loves the city the most, hates the city the most. Whatever. They are the most. Dylan is not the most, nor made for any kind of heat, but has leant in all the same, to the feeling of shedding, continuing to shed, that comes with sweat upon sweat, and summer hair, and summer skin, not quite your own, and cold showers twice a day, washing black sidewalk from sandalled feet, and wet dress against wet breasts, around the block to dry off. Rinse, repeat. Therapeutic to the point it's almost a shame when the weather breaks and she's able to return to the park in midday sun, to watch the usual nothing much September brings, tourists thinning out, everyone trickling back from their summer shares.

She runs her tongue across the last of her double cone and

listens to some guy speak French into his phone, standing like he has a mother that smells good, like some discontinued Dior cologne, like there's a house in the countryside where they all decamp in summer—Arles or Arbres—somewhere plural sounding, ivy up the walls. When he walks on, her eye wanders to a couple on the bench by the dog run.

He, taking a call.

She, pressing a bottle of water to her cheek.

He, calm.

She, flushed, frizzing.

He, Gabe.

She, Kate.

This is shocking. She is shocked. Gabe and Kate out and about inside their day. Inside other days too, presumably, in the two months since bloodied sofa, and blood-filled sneakers, and, *I have a life*, like a gallstone she's yet to pass. A cool, hard roundness, she can pinpoint in her body.

Now Gabe turns his head and reveals an unfamiliar look, clean-shaven, but for a sad strip of hair—a pencil moustache, is it? A creeping heat begins to register at the back of her neck, a blushing kind of heat that understands she is in some way implicated in this absurd development. And, even as blushing turns to burning, she's begun the work of filling in, this thing on Gabe's face. One side longer than the other, she's picturing, up close; reedy, but charged, like a snapped thermometer, all his mercury burrowing sideways. And she thinks of his white feet in summer, taped heels in damp espadrilles, the way he grunts when he comes, and, *Don't hide from me baby*, that time she slipped out to brush her teeth—head cocked, legs dropped open in five A.M. light. And only now does it occur to her how desire can be manufactured from nothing, from mild repulsion, even. And what power there is in this. In how incidental the fact of Gabe. In this creative energy being hers alone, constantly renewing. Cunning the way this works.

The way a Gabe can work; a city.

She tongues the pretzel at the bottom of her cone and watches as Kate stoops to retrieve the thing that has rolled from her bag—an orange?—now stopping at Gabe's foot, which he doesn't move, until the moment Kate stands to walk over.

Kate does not react when the orange rolls past her, only turns to pick it up, then sits again, several feet from Gabe.

Gabe finishes his call, then shifts his weight in a way that makes him seem to hang, just slightly, over his side of the bench.

Kate moves her bag from one side of her to the other, then back again, which is when Gabe tries to cross his legs and is stopped by the trash can on his left, a broken vendor's umbrella perched inside it, like a wrong piña colada.

For a long time, she has wanted something to happen to these people; for this to be cruel and unusual. But it's laughter that comes watching their broken choreography, system still rebooting. Or else this is what the system looks like when it's working?

After the laughter comes something like sympathy.

Or empathy, is it?

Control gone missing from all of them.

She leaves the two of them unspooling, like the trailer for a movie she's seen, or can guess at quite easily. After Waverley, she takes Grove, West Fourth, Charles, where the sound of distant thunder begins to roll. She picks up her pace crossing Hudson and is struck by the thing she used to feel all the time, which is the profound thrill of the ordinary in New York City. The impossible romance of carrying a grocery bag down a city block. Of reheeling a boot or cutting a key. Of having a key to cut. Of being right on the cusp of fall, and skies that go on for ever, and clouds that seem to pass through towers, and crisp, brisk knits and roasted pretzel, and ochre sidewalk, ginkgo trim, and the whole city holding its breath, it feels like; that low-grade ache set to high, that is the pleasure and pain of loving a thing you are certain, at some point, to lose.

A person would have to be crazy to leave New York, the whole city's thinking, in fall. And yet she is certain she can do without it. Certain enough to place a bet on herself without its scaffold, for now, at least. See if she holds up.

She climbs her stoop and sits.

Licks the dust from a pink stick of gum.

Waits for the rain to come.

ACCORD, NY

Snow this morning, a double dump.

The sky, vague for days, suddenly clear, like a smacked TV. Below this, total white-out, a cosmic correction. Easier against this backdrop to see whatever danger she'd imagined when she first arrived, pictured separating from the treeline, or worse still, already at the cabin, pressed up against the glass.

Nothing like this, of course.

No one watching.

A kind of self-surveillance has emerged in its place, not the usual imagining herself from the outside, how she might seem, here, now, in this place, but trained squarely on the fact of her. How she is knitted together, the shapes she makes in the course of a day, rolling on thermals, reaching for logs, bending to write. How these shapes knit into sequences. The way leg attaches to hip, and rolls to make walking, each morning to a different part of Accord, then back to the cabin. Each loop part of a bigger shape she is making, but cannot see.

She touches her fingers to the glass door, everything beyond made surface. Wild to think this is still New York, the city only a few hours away, buried too, if only for a moment, before snow mowers sending up white arches, monstrous ploughs surfacing Fifth, Madison, Lex, like the bones of some T-Rex.

Not so here.

Here, total submission.

Deafening sound of stopped snow.

Pleasing, how it holds its shape, when she slides the door open, like cake slipped from the tin. She takes a lungful of air, lets it burn, and feels again the thing she's been feeling for a while, up here. Which is mad with space. She feels mad with space, and the trick, she's learning, is to leave it alone. Not to force portals or openings. Not to aggrandise or mythologise. Only to let it fill her up; leave stretchmarks.

Unsustainable in the long run, of course. Life waiting to pile back in. But here, in this moment, she can make the choice. And again tomorrow. And the day after that. To be mad with space. A loose end, sparking.

To let herself happen.

Acknowledgements

For her wisdom and generosity, I am forever grateful to Tessa Hadley, without whom this book would not have happened.

I thank Ana Fletcher and Anna Webber for giving me a chance so early on, and for their unwavering support since then.

I'm immensely grateful to everyone at Jonathan Cape and Vintage. To Michal Shavit and Željka Marošević for their flawless taste and editorial guidance; to Alison Tulett and Leah Boulton for going above and beyond; and to Suzanne Dean, for my extraordinary cover design.

All writing comes from reading, and my great thanks go to Hugh and Rosemary Pountney, David Cohen, Sam Fraser and Lucy Newlyn for the impact they had on my relationship with books growing up. I owe them so much.

I would be nowhere without the army of friends and relatives that have always had my back—I thank them all. In writing this book, particular thanks go to Ale Klein and Dani Crocco for our shared New York, to Rick Clapp for those first unrepeatable years, and to Alison Burns for the gift of the city, and so much more. Back in London, my very special thanks go to Stuart Valentine for his million casual acts of generosity, and to Lucy Clayton for decades of joyous wanging on about doing something like this, then both finally doing it.

My monstrous thanks to the Bens. Benj Fleetwood Smyth, for a best friendship that's truly one for the ages; Benedict Morrison, for the endless inspiration; and Ben Pountney, for loving our family and for my excellent nephew, Jacob.

This book owes a great debt to the MA in Creative Writing at Bath Spa, for a dream year of focus and encouragement, and for the gift of Sarah Deacon and Camilla Doherty—two talented writers whose ongoing support has meant everything. Sarah especially, I cannot thank you enough for the endless calls, meals and late-night reality checks. Thanks also to writer Gavin Plumley for so generously sharing his own experience of publication, and for many years of fine friendship.

My beloved father died very suddenly a few months ago. I don't know a better, more charismatic person—a lover of life, of words and of his family. Above all, I want to thank him and my wonderful mother for their unconditional support; for living such rich lives before they met; for all the sacrifice since then; for the great adventure they made of my childhood; and for providing a home where I've always felt totally safe. It's impossible to overstate my love, gratitude and admiration for you both. Anything I've achieved, I owe to you.

And Pa, I'm sorry I took so long to finish this. I'll miss you forever.

My profound thanks go to Stephen Sondheim for his lyrics to 'Beautiful' from *Sunday in the Park with George*; to *New York* magazine for the creatures mentioned in its 2009 article 'Secrets of the Deep'; to Livescience.com for its facts on the mating rituals of crabs; to PJ Johnson for lines from their poem 'Alice'; and to Clarice Lispector for quotations from her novel *Água Viva*.

Miranda Pountney is a writer based in London. She holds a BA in English Literature from Oxford University and an MA in Creative Writing from Bath Spa University. *How to Be Somebody Else* is her first novel.